RED FLEECE

WILL LEVINGTON COMFORT

1st WORLD
LIBRARY
Literary Society

Red Fleece

Will Levington Comfort

© 1st World Library, 2007
PO Box 2211
Fairfield, IA 52556
www.1stworldlibrary.com
First Edition

LCCN: 2007927861

Softcover ISBN: 978-1-4218-4583-8
Hardcover ISBN: 978-1-4218-4499-2
eBook ISBN: 978-1-4218-4667-5

Purchase *"Red Fleece"*
as a traditional bound book at:
www.1stWorldLibrary.com/purchase.asp?ISBN=978-1-4218-4583-8

1st World Library is a literary, educational organization dedicated to:

- Creating a free internet library of downloadable ebooks

- Hosting writing competitions and offering book publishing scholarships.

Interested in more 1st World Library books? contact:
literacy@1stworldlibrary.com
Check us out at: www.1stworldlibrary.com

1st World Library Literary Society

Giving Back to the World

"If you want to work on the core problem, it's early school literacy."

- James Barksdale, former CEO of Netscape

"No skill is more crucial to the future of a child, or to a democratic and prosperous society, than literacy."

- Los Angeles Times

"Literacy... means far more than learning how to read and write... The aim is to transmit... knowledge and promote social participation."

- UNESCO

"Literacy is not a luxury, it is a right and a responsibility. If our world is to meet the challenges of the twenty-first century we must harness the energy and creativity of all our citizens."

- President Bill Clinton

"Parents should be encouraged to read to their children, and teachers should be equipped with all available techniques for teaching literacy, so the varying needs and capacities of individual kids can be taken into account."

- Hugh Mackay

TO THE HOUR—WHEN TROOPS TURN HOME

CONTENTS

I

THE WOMAN AND THE EXILE

Peter Mowbray first saw her at the corner of Palace Square nearest the river. He was not in the least the kind of young man who appraises passing women, very far from a starer. At the instant their eyes met, his thoughts had been occupied with work matters and the trickery of events. In fact, there was so much to do that he resented the intrusion, found himself hoping in the first flash that she would show some flaw to break the attraction.

It may have been that her eyes were called to the passer-by just as his had been, without warning or volition. In any event their eyes met full, leisurely in that stirring silence before the consciousness of self, time, place and convention rushes in. ... Though she seemed very poor, there was something about her beyond reach in nobility. He was left with the impression of the whitest skin, the blackest hair and the reddest lips, but mainly of a gray-eyed girl—eyes that had become wider and wider, and had filled with sudden amazement (doubtless at her own answering look) before they turned away.

Desolation was abroad in Warsaw after this encounter. Mowbray thought of New York with loneliness, the zest gone from all present activity. Presently with curious grip his thoughts returned to a certain luncheon in New York with a tired literary man who had talked about women with the air of a connoisseur. The pith of the writer's observations was restored to his mind in this form:

"If I were to marry again it would be to a Latin woman— French, Italian, even Spanish—a close-to-nature woman born and bred in one of the Mediterranean countries. Not a blue-blood, for that has to do with decadence, but a woman of the people. They are passionate but pure, as Poe would say. If they find a man of any value, he becomes their world. They are strong natural mothers—mothering their children and their husband, too,—and immune to common sicknesses. Given a little food, they know enough to prepare it with art. If a man has a bit of a dream left, such a woman will either make him forget it painlessly, or she will make it come true."

There was no apparent relation, and none that proved afterward. What he had seen at the corner of Palace Square nearest the Vistula was not the face of a Latin woman, nor was any looseness of common birth evident in it. The key might have had to do with the little hat she wore, just a hat for wearing on the head, a protection against sun and rain, and with the austerely simple black dress; but these weathered exteriors again were effective in contrast to the vivid freshness of her natural coloring. As for what remained of the literary man's picture of the ideal woman to marry, it was the last word of decadence—the eminent selfishness of a man willing to accept the luxury of a woman who asks little to be happy. ... The next day at the same time and place Mowbray was there, and saw her coming from afar.

She seemed both afraid and angry, stopped abruptly and asked in Polish what he wanted. He was startled. It was a hard moment. He explained with difficulty that her language

Will Levington Comfort

was as yet an inconvenient vehicle for him.

"You are not Russian?" she said in French.

He shook his head. She seemed to be relieved and he wondered why.

"What do you want?" she asked, though not quite with the original asperity.

"It did not occur to me you would notice," he said in the language she had ventured. "I saw you yesterday. You made me think of New York. As I was near to-day, I hoped to see you again—" "You are American?" She spoke now in English, and with a still softer intonation.

"Yes,—you speak English, too?"

"I like it. It is—" she checked herself and asked with just a shade of coldness, "Is there anything I can do for you?"

It might be construed as a courtesy to a stranger from one who lived in Warsaw. Peter liked it, a certain vista opening. However, there was no answer within reach except the truth, and he plunged:

"I should like to know you better."

The red lower lip disappeared beneath the other. Her gray eyes grew very wide; something intrepid and exquisite in her manner as she searched his face. Whatever she knew of the world, she dared still to trust her intuition—this was something of the revelation he drew.

"Why?"

Many people were passing. He looked toward the quieter center of the Square.

"Will you walk with me there?" he asked. "It is not easy to explain this sort of thing—"

"No. I must go on. You may walk a little way."

"You are very good.... You see, I cannot tell just *why*—as you asked. If I knew you well, I could tell you. Yesterday I was quite unromantic—"

She made it hard for him and did not let him see her smile. "You mean you are romantic to-day?"

Peter laughed. "What a trap—and I was trying so hard to tell you."

"You *were* trying—"

"I don't need to tell you. All there is to say is that I want you to be my friend."

"I should have to think," she answered.

"Of course. ... Do you pass here every day?"

"I should have to think," she said.

It was the third day afterward that she passed again.

Will Levington Comfort

Chapter 2

The first time that Boylan of the *Rhodes News Agency* of New York saw Peter Mowbray was in the office of Lonegan of *The States*, Mowbray's chief in Warsaw. Lonegan had known Peter in New York and had wanted him for his second many months before the fact was brought about. This was the Boylan of the Schmedding Polar Failure, of various wars and expeditions, a huge spectacle of a man, an old-timer, and very fond of Lonegan, though as representative of *Rhodes'* he was structurally the competitor of *The States* in this territory.

"Young Mowbray may be all right," Boylan observed, "but the curse of the student is on him. I should say that he isn't gusty enough for hard work—vest buttons too safe—"

"You can't measure health by the pound," Lonegan observed, regarding the other's bulk with one eye shut. "I never heard of Mowbray spending much time in bed outside of the small hours." "How old is he?" "Twenty-six or seven."

"I suppose he put on his gear all in a year or two?"

"There is that look about him, but he's safely over it. Some people never stop, but I've had to look up at him from the same angle now and then during the last five years.... It was just a little before that he happened into—his route like mine—his cub-year in London, then assistant in Antwerp, then in Dresden. He had Dresden alone for a year. I've been angling for him some time—"

"Yes," Boylan remarked, "you need the right kind of help to stand up with *Rhodes* from this end—"

"You do make it wildly exciting," Lonegan answered gently. "We'll rock Peter yet."

This chat took place in June. Ten weeks afterward Boylan came in with the big news, and found Lonegan bending over the following cablegram, almost the last that came through in the private cipher of *The States:*

Get Mowbray post with Russians. We are mailing influential matters. Warsaw key-desk for northern campaigns. We are to be congratulated on having Lonegan there.

It was from the Old Man, who in certain cases ventured thus to be expensively felicitous....

"I'm sorry, Lonegan," Boylan said. "I thought you would be taking the field—"

"No, the Old Man's got the right eye for these affairs. I'm a desk man."

What Lonegan had swallowed to make his voice clear and steady, only he knew, but his nerve was effective. "You've got to help me, Boylan," he said. "You know the military end. You've got to help me get him attached. I know you'd do it for me, but I want you to do it for him—"

A grunt from the big man, who disappeared.

...Lonegan's lip curled. Again it was only Lonegan who knew why. He read the cablegram carefully again, and felt his face as if speculating whether he could wait until morning for a shave. There was routine to do, and the developments of the day to file. Peter was on a mail story.... It occurred to him presently that his second would be interested in this eventuality from the Office. He called several places by

Will Levington Comfort

'phone without locating the younger man.

"He's with the woman," Lonegan concluded.

Peter had left her address somewhere, but it was not at hand; neither was her house available to telephone. Lonegan took down the Warsaw directory, and came finally to the street-number after this line:

"Bertha Solwicz, sempstress."

Chapter 3

She, too, was almost a stranger in Warsaw, and lonely. Each had their work, and many hours each day were required for it; still, after the first fortnight, they managed to meet often. Peter's time was hers, for he had the habit of leaving his feature-letter for the quiet hours of the night.

"I hate the name of Solwicz," she told him the first time he came to her house, "especially from you. And you must call me *Berthe*, not Bertha." In spite of her obvious lack of means, she had a few friends of rare quality, and yet he did not meet them. On her table that first day, he picked up a little book of poems, the leader of which was entitled *We Are Free*. Peter had read it a few weeks before and given it a quality of appreciation that was seldom called in these days. Just now he noted that the volume was affectionately inscribed to her from the author, Moritz Abel. She spoke of him and of the group of young master workmen to which he belonged. Then she read the poem, as they stood together. It was a moment of honor to the poet. Peter had turned pale, and the little room was hushed about them, as if Warsaw were suddenly stilled.

"You see what they are doing," she said. "There is a new race of artists in Russia. They have passed the emotions—"

"This poem was due in the world," Peter said. "But it is still an age ahead of the crowd."

"That's what makes it so hard for them—for him. He does not like that. He would like to talk to all men straight. Moritz Abel—the name will not be forgotten. He is like the others of the new race. They are terrible in their calm. They have passed the emotions. They are free. Other artists in Europe or

Will Levington Comfort

America repress the emotions. That is but the beginning of the mastery. When they are as great as this group of young men, they will show the spirit of the thing, not the emotion of it. Emotions are red. This is pure white, don't you see?"

For three days Warsaw had been upheaved in excitement. On the afternoon that the messenger from Lonegan brought the news of the cablegram, Berthe and Peter were planning an excursion into the country for the next day. She watched him closely as he read, and was sensitive enough to realize the importance of the message, before he spoke.... He found her gray eyes upon him. She chose her own way to break the tension:

"The country is heaven, no doubt about that. One must die to get there. Also one must live just so. Even when I was little, something always happened—just as we were planning to set out for the country."

He showed her the message, but had hardly heard her words. His discovery of this slender solitary red-lipped girl and what it meant, was rarely clear at this moment. She had awakened him plane by plane, awakened his passion and his mercy and his intuition.

"Tell me again what you said about the country. I was away for a minute."

"It is hard to think of a little excursion to the fields—with such a holiday ahead, as you are called upon."

"I wasn't thinking of that either, Berthe, but of you."

"Of course, you will go?"

"Doubtless."

"I was only talking foolishly, about our little excursion. One's own wants are so pitifully unimportant now."

"I had hardly expected personally to encounter a war," he remarked and added smilingly, "The fact is, I hadn't thought of meeting a woman like you."

"I don't believe you're as cold-blooded as you try to seem, Peter."

"I have fought all my life to be cold-blooded."

She never forgot that. "I wonder why men do it?"

"It's the cultivation, perhaps, of that which Americans love best of all—"

"What?"

"Nerve."

"We of Poland dare to be emotional," she said.

"You are an older people. You know how."

"One needs only to be one's self."

Peter smiled. "Sometimes I dare actually to be honest with you. Even Lonegan and I take no such liberties together."

"It isn't a matter of courage," she said. "You would dare anything. I know your quiet, deadly kind of courage. That's the first thing I felt about you."

It was like Mowbray not to acknowledge that such a thing had been said.

"I came to you asleep. I wonder if I should always have remained asleep?"

"Your words are pretty, Peter. It makes me sad that you are going away."

"You remember that company of soldiers that passed us yesterday as we walked? I had seen many such groups before—great shocky-haired fellows who ate and drank disgustingly. But yesterday you made me see that their blood is redder than the Little Father's—that empires ripen and go to seed only on a grander scale than turnips." Her eyes were gleaming.

"We who are so wise, who have mastered ourselves, should be very good to the peasants—and not take what they have and kill them in wars."

"Did I lead you to believe in any way that I felt myself mastered?" he asked quickly.

She touched his arm. "I was talking of the Fatherland," she answered.

He had met this intensity of hers before. Her scorn was neither hot nor cold, but electric. So often when words failed her, Peter fancied himself lost in some superb wilderness... Her own gray tone was in the room to-day—her gray eyes and black hair that made the shadows seem gray; her face that no night could hide from him. Sometimes his glance was held to her lips—as one turns to the firelight. Passion there— or was it the higher thing, *compassion?* There was bend and give to the black cloth she wore, as to the inflections of her voice. She could forget herself. That was the first and the inexhaustible charm.

It is true that she was very poor. This room which had become his sanctuary in Warsaw was in a humble house of a common quarter. She laughed at this, and at her many hours of work each day, for which the return was meager. There was the sweetest pathos to him in her little purse, and her pride in these matters was a thing of royalty.

"My father earned the right to be poor," she once said.

It seemed to him that her father was mentioned in the moments most memorable... She was at the window now, her hand lifting the shade. The light of the gray day shone through her fingers—a long, fragile hand that trembled.

"Shall we walk somewhere, or must you go to your office, Peter?"

"I won't, just yet. Yes, let's go outside."

They felt they must climb, a bit of suffocation in their hearts. Until to-day there had been invariable stimulus for Mowbray in the age of all things, even in the dusty, narrow, lower streets, but his smiling, easy countenance was a lie that he disliked now. It pinched him cruelly to leave her, and there was small amelioration in anything that the war might bring. She would give him sympathy and zeal and honor for the work and through all the lonely days, but what a lack would be of that swift directness of purpose, the deeper seeing, the glad capacity for higher heroism which he had found only in her presence. They crossed the riverward corner of the Square, where they had met. He tried to tell her how she had seemed that first day.

"I cannot understand," she replied. "Especially that day when I first saw you, I had nothing."

Now they ascended the terraces that commanded the Vistula. The rocky turf of the footpath, smoothed by the tread of forgotten generations (but still whispering to her of those who had passed on); the crumbling masonry of the retaining walls, gray with the pallor of the years; and afar the curving, dust-swept farmlands, which had mothered a thousand harvests, now moved with strange planting of peasant-soldiers. Mobilization business everywhere, drilling of the half-equipped, a singing excitement of parting, recruiting—no time for the actual misery.

They stood in the very frown of the fortress at sunset. A column of raw infantry came swinging out and started the descent. A moment afterward the roar of a folk-song came up in a gust. It was as if the underworld suddenly had been cratered.

"When they sing like that, and I think of what they shall soon be called upon to do—I can hardly endure it!" she whispered.... They stood with backs against the wall, as the tail of the column moved past. "Look at that weary one—so spent and sick—yet trying to sing—"

They were in the silence again. Across the river, against the red background, they watched another column of foot-soldiers moving like a procession of ants erect; and beyond, on the dim plain, a field battery, just replenished to war footing, was toiling with tired beasts and untried pieces. Mowbray thought of the human meat being herded in Austria for those great rakish guns, as the infantry below was being trained for distant slaughter arenas.

"Do speak, Peter," she whispered.

He turned to find her white face looking up to him and very close. They were alone.

"You won't mind if I think about myself this once?" he asked.

"Please do."

"I only want to say that, if you'll stay where you are, I'll come back from this stuff—I was going to say, dead or alive."

"Do you mean I am to stay in Warsaw?" she asked.

"No—not that exactly. I mean if you will stay where you are in regard to me—"

Tears filled her eyes. He would have known it even if they had not shone through the dusk, because his fingers felt the tremor in her arms. She tried to speak, but finished, "How utterly silly words are!"

The face of young Mowbray was strange with emotion, pale but brilliant-eyed, his long features bending to her. She was utter receptivity. Neither knew until afterward how rare and perfect was this moment.

"Anyway—we understand. We understand, Berthe."

"...As for Berthe," she said slowly, as they walked back, "her heart will stay where you have put it, Peter. That's out of her power to change. But the rest—I can't tell, yet—"

It was as if a finger had crossed Mowbray's face laterally under the eyes and across his nostrils, leaving a gray welt.

"I know you belong to the moderns," he said, after a moment. "We men belong to the ancients. We want a woman to wait and weep while we go off to the wars."

"We understand," she kept repeating.... "And now, before you go, come home with me and let me make you a cup of tea—just a cup of tea—before you go."

He went with her, and, when his tea-cup was finished, he happened to look into the bottom.

"What do you see?" she asked quickly, taking the cup.

"M-m-m," said Mowbray.

Chapter 4

Peter and Lonegan were together at dinner three hours after the message from *The States*.

"It's a big chance, Mowbray. That's all I can say. I stay at the wire—no heroics."

"You ought to see it all from here."

Lonegan smiled deprecatingly. "Boylan will help you get through. You don't know him yet. Some time, perhaps, you will—two hundred and fifty pounds of soul. He'll do all he can to get you the same chance he has, because I asked him; and then he'll try to make *The States* look obsolete as a newspaper, wherein, of course, he'll fail. But he'll try. If he takes to you, it won't make him try less, but he'd do your stuff and his, if you fell sick. There isn't another Boylan—a great newspaper man, too. *The States* will watch closely, knowing that *Rhodes'* will get everything possible from Boylan's part of the front. The point is—and I think he'll want it, too—you'd better work together on the main line of stuff, as we do here. Your letters on the side should be better than his, because you're a better writer. As for war stuff, Boylan is the old master—Peking, Manchuria and the Balkans—that I think of; also the Schmedding Polar Failure. That last *was* war—a spectacular expedition of the Germans—

"I might as well make this a lecture, now that I've started," Lonegan went on. "The war game isn't complex. All the bewildering technicalities that bristle from a military officer's talk are just big-name stuff designed to keep down the contempt of the crowd—the oldest professional trick. Whenever the crowd gets to understand your terminology

Will Levington Comfort

your game is cooked. You know how it is in a drug-store, and you've seen the old family doctor look wise....

"There's a lot of different explosives which they fire by mathematics, and which you can learn in part from our homely encyclopedias, but the main game will be fought out on the same principles that Attila fought it and Genghis Khan—numbers, traps, unexpectedness, the same dull old flanking activities, the raid of supplies and communications, the bending back of wings, the crimp of a line by making a hole in one part—and all that archaic rot. As I say, the game is extinct, so far as our modern complicated intelligences go, and the men whose names are biggest in the papers from now on are the same old beefy type of rudiments whom a man wouldn't associate with in times of national quiet.... I will end this by saying that the big story is the man—the peasant, the trooper, the one blinded little dupe, who dies, or plunges, or loses his legs in the name of the Fatherland—"

"I see that," said Peter; "but what really is interesting to me is this peasant's blindness and the monkey other men make of him—"

"I'm glad you spoke of that, for it is a thing to avoid. Interesting, I grant, but not popular with our kind of press. We are not servants of the minority or the elect. You'll find Boylan exploiting the army he's with—just as another might have done under Napoleon. By the way, where are you going to-night?"

"I'm going to sit at the feet of the most genial anarchist at large. His name is Fallows, an American, who has been ten years in Russia among the peasants."

"Duke Fallows—I know of him. When did he come to town?"

"Two days ago."

"Peter, how did you get next?" Lonegan looked a bit in awe at the other.

"I was asked to one of his private audiences last night."

Peter knew that Lonegan had many things to ask by the quick tone in which he spoke the first question.

"You know what Fallows will do to you?"

"Yes, if one lets go. He has learned how to use his power. He has brought forth his young upon the bare rocks, as somebody said."

"He'd turn an angel into an anarchist."

"A man ought not to be afraid to listen if there's a chance for him to be proved wrong—"

"Correct, absolutely. I am merely thinking about our job."

"A man gets in the habit of thinking about his job—doesn't he?"

"Did he tell you about the plowman of Liaoyang?"

"No, but my companion did. Fallows must have seen that episode rather clearly."

"Let's not get off the job business, Peter. As I was saying, the truth isn't popular—"

"That doesn't sound like Lonegan."

"No, and I don't like the feel of saying it, but it's very much to the point—"

"Possibly."

"Mowbray, we are taking our bread, and its cake, too, from a paper that expects us to exploit the orthodox heroics. The pity and atrocious sham of it all has its side. But the fact still remains its side does not furnish the stuff that American newspapers pay men and cable tolls to furnish."

"Won't you come to-night?" Peter asked laughing. "Perhaps we can both reach the high point some day when we have earned the right to be poor."

"That's a higher point than I dream of, Peter. I can't help but think what a nest you've got into. Of course, I mean with Fallows and his kind—"

"An eagle's nest."

"But the eaglets are starving."

"Heretofore the job has been served. Come along with me and meet Duke Fallows again—"

"No. I must go back to the wire for the present. Boylan would be shocked, too. By the way, I've got a bid in for you with General Kohlvihr. Boylan is to help me put it through, of course. The more decorated they are the more they fall for Boylan. There's a chance that you'll start south with a column within two days. So you'd better get at that encyclopedia stuff—"

"Yes, I'll attend to that."

Peter left him smiling, and turned his steps across the Square, into a narrow street of the poor quarter, and on toward a little room and a low lamp, where a woman's hands sewed magically as she waited.

Will Levington Comfort

Chapter 5

Fallows met them in his small bleak room, turned the lamp low, and opened the door of the diminutive wood-stove to let the firelight in the room. The three sat around it.... Peter Mowbray felt strange and young beside them. The woman seemed to belong to this world, and it was a world at war with every existing power. All Peter's training resisted stubbornly. Still, right or wrong, there was a nobility about their stand. He did not need to be sure their vision was absolutely true, yet the suspicion developed that they saw more clearly than he, and acted more purely. Mowbray did not lack anything of valor, but he lacked the fire somehow. He loved Berthe Solwicz, could have made every sacrifice for her, but that was a concrete thing.

Fallow's bony knees were close to the fire. He seemed both light and deep, often turning to Peter with secret intentness, and openly regarding the young woman with amazement and delight. Nearing fifty, Fallows was tall, thin and tanned. The deep lines of his face were those which make a man look homely to himself, but often interesting to others. His soft, low-collared shirt was somewhat of a spectacle in consideration of the angular and weathered neck. No rest could exist in the room that contained such loneliness as burned from his eyes. It was said that he had been rich, though everything about him was poor now. One would suspect the articles in his pockets to be meager and of poor quality—the things you might find in a peasant's coat. That which he called home was a peasant's house in the Bosk hills—the house of the plowman of Liaoyang, whose children he fathered. Annually, however, he went abroad, telling the story of the underdog, usually making the big circuit from the East to the West, and stopping at a certain little cabin within hearing distance of the whistles of Manhattan, where his first disciple worked in solitude mainly, and against the stream. Just now Fallows was planning a different winter's work.... They talked of the first fighting.

"The startling thing to realize is that for the present we are allied with England," said Fallows. "I mean Russia. You see, I am Russian, now, not the Russia of the Bear, but of the Man—"

Mowbray and the woman exchanged glances, each thinking of the tea-cup in the afternoon.... The exile showed traces of his ten years' training among simple men. Rhetoric and dithyramb were gone from his speech and habit of mind. The whole study and vision of the man was to make his words plain. Thus he said slowly:

"The peasants are children—children in mind and soul. We who have come a little farther are responsible for them, as a father is responsible for his children. So far we have wronged them, taught them to grasp instead of to give, to look down instead of up. We have even stolen from them the fruits of their looking down. The time is near at hand when we shall have to pay for all this.... A true father would die for his children. I know men who have done that, and there are men about us here, even in Warsaw tonight, who are ready for that—"

Fallows' voice was tender. He watched the face of the woman as he spoke. She was looking hard into the fire.

Fallows added: "There are fifty million men here in Russia— roughly speaking. Very strong, very simple, possibly very brutal men, but brutal as a fine dog is brutal, a simplicity about that. I do not idealize them. I have lived among them. I know this: They might be led to virtue, instead of to wickedness. My heart bleeds for them being led to slaughter again.

The hard thing is to make them see, but the reason for that is simple, too. If they could see—they would not be children. They must be led. Never in modern history have they been purely led. Words cannot make them see; wars so far have not made them see. It may be that the sufferings and heroisms of this war shall be great enough to make them see...."

"What would you have the peasants see first?" Peter asked.

"Their real fathers—that men of wisdom and genius are the true fathers of the Fatherland, not the groups of predatory men. True fathers would die for their children. To me it has been blasphemy, when the nations of the past have called themselves Fatherlands. I would have the peasants fathered by men who realize that the peasants are the strength and salt of the earth; men who realize that the plan of life is good— that the plan of life is for concord and service each to the other—that the hate of man for man is the deadly sin, the hell of the world—that the fields and all the treasures of the mother earth are for those who serve and aspire, and not for those who hold fast, look down and covet more."

Mowbray was interested in the fact that Fallows had passed the stage of eloquence and scorn and burning hatred against evil in persons and institutions. There was no hue and cry about his convictions. He seemed to live in continual amazement at the slowness with which the world moves— the slowness to a man who is ahead and trying to pull his people along. Moreover there was that final wisdom which Fallows revealed from time to time—momentary loss of the conviction that he himself was immortally right. Fallows saw, indeed, that a man may be atrociously out of plumb, even to the point of becoming a private and public nuisance, when allowed to feed too long alone on the strong diet of his own convictions.... An hour sped by. Fallows replenished the fire and turned to Berthe Solwicz.

"All evening you've had something in your mind to tell me and I've been giving forth. You must forgive a man for so many words—when he has been living with little children so long. What is it?"

"Just a reading of a tea-cup to-day—but everything you said has its meaning concerned in it."

"I'm almost as interested in tea-cups as in the stars," said Fallows.

"You know a toy-bear, such as the Germans make?"

"Yes—"

"Well, it would have been like that—if one were thinking of toys. We thought of the Russian Bear. It was perfect—in the bottom of the cup—standing up, walking like a man—huge paunch, thick paws held out pathetically, legs stretched out, just as he would be, rocking, you know—"

Fallows bowed seriously. Mowbray turned his smile to the shadows.

"Near him," Berthe added, "was a Russian soldier—perfect —fur cap, high boots, tightly belted, very natty—more perfect than we see in the streets, as if drawn from ideal. He was stabbing the bear with a long pole, leisurely—"

"It was a rifle and bayonet," said Peter. "We both saw it, but didn't speak until now. He was churning the bayonet around in the great paunch as if feeling for the vitals. The bear looked large and helpless."

Fallows' bronzed head had sunk upon his chest. His eyes, red with firelight, seemed lost to all expression. "I was thinking it would happen in Germany first," he said.

A moment afterward he added: "There's a time when a man wants to die for what he believes, and another time when he's afraid he will die before he gets a chance to make his life count."

Again he paused, and then looked up to Mowbray. "It's a good omen. That's the *real* war.... And was it your cup?"

"Yes."

"You say that you are going out for the Galician service?"

"Yes, possibly with Kohlvihr's column."

"You will see much service," said Fallows. "That used to be our dream—to see service. It will be easier seen with the Russians. They are not so modern in method as the French or Germans, or even the Japanese. Of course, war is the same. The nation at the end will win on the fields, not in the skies. The sky fulfillment is reserved for a better utility than war. But war belongs under the sea.... You will not be suppressed so rigidly with the Russians. You will see the side of the war which will have the most bearing on the future. I do not believe France and Germany are in the future as Russia is—"

"And England?" Peter asked quickly.

"The key to that is the wealth of the Indies—as of yore."

"You mean if India remains loyal?"

"If India remains under the yoke."

"But, if Britain should preserve her tenure in India with the Japanese troops—" Peter suggested.

Fallows shuddered. "As yet I can see no philosophy under heaven to cover that."

"And you think Britain and Russia are enemies in spite of this alliance?"

"Enemies, temperamental and structural—enemies, past and future."

Peter recurred to this point: "You think that India would not remain loyal if she had arms?"

"I was in a little village of the Punjab two years ago," Fallows replied, "and there was a lad of sixteen there, wonderful in promise—a mind, a spirit. They could not raise in the village enough money to send him across the seas steerage for his education. A single rifle costs nearly three pounds. It is hard for us to realize how poor India is."

Peter stood fast against this in his mind; his intellect would not accept.... "Are you going to take the field again, Mr. Fallows?"

"Not in a newspaper way. I shall nurse wounded soldiers. At least they have accepted me.... These are fearful and amazing days. We have all been in a kind of long feeding dream, like the insects, accumulating energy and terrible power for these days. Such death as we shall see!"

There was silence.

"I wonder how they are taking it in America?" Fallows mused.

"Doubtless as an opportunity for world-trade," said Peter.

"Oh, I hope not!" the exile said passionately. "There must be another America."

Fallows placed his hands on Berthe's shoulders, looking down: "You make me think of a young woman I once knew," he said. "Not that you look like her—but that you have the same zeal *for something*.... You are a very true daughter of your father—"

"You knew him?" she said huskily.

"We all knew him—we who dare to think we look ahead. When he died, his courage came to all of us. We were changed. If it had not been a pure and durable thing—his courage would have died with him. It is wonderful for me to be here with you. And this man loves you."

It was not a question, just a fragmentary utterance of a fine moment. Fallows said it as a man who has passed on, and yet loves to study the lives and loves of younger men. Even to Mowbray the feeling came for an instant that he was part of the solution to which they gave themselves.

"I have not told him of my father. He does not know my name," Berthe said. "But I am going to tell him—before he goes."

"He is safe," said Fallows. "I felt free with him—almost immediately—and that picture in the tea-cup!... Peter Mowbray, Peter Mowbray. It is a good name. And you are going out on the big story of the war for *The States*. You will see great things—best of all with the Russian columns. There will be an Austerlitz every day—a Liaoyang every day. I was in Manchuria with a man who made that his battle. I wonder if he will come out this time—to find how his dream of brotherhood is faring? God, how he took to that dream! He will be a Voice—"

They were standing. Fallows suddenly reached for his cap. "I'll go out with you—just to get out. The room is too small for me to-night."

Yet, when they reached the street, he left them abruptly, as if he had already said too much.

"He seems to be burning up," said Peter.

Berthe did not answer.

"He was like Zarathustra coming down from the mountain—so shockingly full of power," Peter added. "And yet he said so little of his own part."

"He couldn't, Peter. He's like you—when moments are biggest.... Oh, Peter, where do you keep your passion?"

"You mean this great burning that Fallows knows?"

"Yes."

"I haven't it. I haven't that passion. I think I am just a reporter. But you have it.... My father loved his family. I think your father must have loved the world—"

"But you love the world—"

"No, I love you."

"Peter, Peter—come to-morrow! Don't come in with me to-night!"

Peter went to his rooms at once. He was struck hard, but merely showed a bit weary. He found himself objecting to characteristics of Fallows' mind, the same which he had admired and delighted in from Berthe. She had always talked easily of death, and he had been without criticism; now he disliked the casual mention of death in Fallows' talk.

Peter saw that he was sore, and hated himself for it. Fallows personally was ready for death; therefore he had the right to counsel martyrdoms for others if he wished. Death to Peter, however, was not strictly a conversational subject. If a man were ready to die for another, it was not good taste to say so. Still he forced himself to be just, by thinking of Fallows' life.

Fallows somehow had turned a corner that he, Peter Mowbray, had not come to so far. Self-hypnotized, or not, the exile had given up everything in life to make the world better as he saw it. He had written and traveled and talked and plotted, even vowed himself to poverty, all for the good of the under-dog.

"It isn't fanaticism, when you come to look at it," Peter mused. "He sees it clearly, and makes one see it for the moment of listening. He isn't afraid. He would die every day for it, if he could.... And I take things as I find them, and grin. I wouldn't even have thought otherwise, except for Berthe. I have a suspicion that I'm half-baked."

Peter's mind was engaging itself thus feverishly, to avoid the main issue that the woman had flung him from her, and run to cover, stuffing her ears, so to speak, and asking him not to follow. He braced himself now and faced it. "If it happened to another pair, I should say it was the finish," he thought. "I should say that no man and woman could pass a rock like that.... I can't get to her point of view by thinking myself there. I'm cold—that's the word. And she's superb. I'd rather be her friend than lord of any other woman. That won't change. And she has spoiled everything I thought I knew. Altogether—it's a game, bright little story—and deep."

Lonegan came in and flung himself down wearily.

"I've been busy. Boylan is leaving in thirty-six hours. You're going with him?"

"I'm ready," said Peter.

"Did you have a big time?"

"Yes."

"What do you think of Fallows now?"

"I'm strong for him."

"Peter—you look bushed."

"It drains a man to spend an evening in that company. A fellow has to have a heavy lid—not to waste fire."

Lonegan was worried. "You don't mean to say you're getting fevers and emotions."

"I'm threatened."

"Mowbray—you're lying. I don't believe you'd let anybody see your fires—not even how well you bank 'em. It isn't in you."

"I wish it were," said Peter.

* * *

For a long time after Lonegan left he plunged into his work, but there was no sleep for him afterward. He lay very still, breathing easily, as the fag-end of the night crawled by. At dawn he arose, dressed noiselessly, and went out into the city.

Chapter 7

It was too early to go to Berthe, yet his steps led him to the street of her house, and he had not passed it a second time before she opened the blinds above, and called to him. He looked at her sorrowfully, and she met his eyes.

"Come in, Peter. I've been so sorry! If you can forgive me, we'll have coffee together—"

He followed her upstairs. The premonition came that he was to take away the image of Berthe Solwicz at its highest—inimitably enticing to his heart, the girlish and utterly feminine spirit that had captivated the man in his breast. She did not seem to know that she was like the woman of the first meeting, but to him all her grace of that day had returned, as if to complete the circle of the episode; and all that he had loved since was added. The one thing in his life that he was proud of, was that he had chosen this woman from the crowd.... They were in her room. With both hands she held him in his coat, so that he could not remove it, begging him to forget the last of last night before they could be at rest.

"I don't know as I want to, Berthe," he said. "It made me think. There are two kinds of people in the world—the kind who give and the kind who take. We represent each. I'm afraid the difference is intrinsic. There would be no satisfaction in me trying to be some one else—even trying to be like you. I am what I am—and must be that. But, Berthe, I can hold the suspicion that I am your inferior, and be pleasant about it—"

"Peter, Peter—you don't understand. I don't love myself—nor my way better. I am poor and tortured, carrying about a legacy, or a dream. I need you. I can tell you now—I never

Will Levington Comfort

needed you so much as last night when I sent you away. I need your brain and balance—your big heart. It was never so dear to me."

This was too much for him. He sat down before her. All night he had been trying to qualify for a lower place in her heart than his earlier dreams had called for—any place rather than to be apart—for the stuff of adoration was in Peter Mowbray. Half-sitting, half-kneeling, she took her place on the rug before him.

"But first I must tell you the story. I could not tell you at once; and since then we have managed so well. But you must know before you go. I am not Polish, not even in name. My father's mother was a Russian woman, but his father was an Irishman, and the name—my name—is Wyndham. My father's given name was 'Metz'—"

Peter had caught it all before her last sentence. "Wyndham" had been enough. He saw clearly the natural and excellent reason for the tenderness of Duke Fallows toward the daughter of Metz Wyndham, and recalled the tragic story of the power and fire of this prophet of the people, who was executed by the Russian government in the midst of the turmoil following Red Sunday—"Metz Wyndham, the notorious Red," as he was denoted in the subsidized press of Petersburg, though "Metz Wyndham, the peasants' martyr," was a whisper which seemed destined in the end to silence all such uproar.

"You have heard of him? You knew his story?"

The upturned face shone with a different bloom for his eyes. "Yes," he answered.

"...I was away from Russia for years—in London and Paris,"

she said quickly. "But at last I felt I could not stay longer. I wanted to come back here—where the struggle is so tense and constant. He worked much here in Warsaw. All of his kind come some time to Warsaw. And so the name *Solwicz*, which I hate; and so the fear when I found you watching me in the street a second time, and my relief to learn that you were not Russian-"

"Of course I understand," said Peter. He put his hand upon her head. "I was in awe of you before I knew," he added, "and yet, I always saw that in the most vital moments something of him would come out.... I keep seeing you with him now—what a life for a young girl—what a builder, those years, for a young girl—and how brave you are. Berthe, I have it—you are spoiled for common people because you were brought up with that kind of a man. How clearly I understand last night now!"

"There's another side to that," she said huskily.

"Oh, I'm sorry—"

The most consummate plotting could not have endeared him to her as those three words.

"Peter, you must see it—the other side. There was no rest with him. All his brilliance, all his brilliant companions were one part, but there was a steady pressure of tragedy about us—from outside. And there was tragic pressure from him. He was subject to the most terrible melancholia. He had enough vision to see the wrong everywhere. It was not mania. There *is* wrong everywhere, if one looks—in judges and cities, in nations, wars, in the kind of amusements people plunge into—wrong and coarseness and stupidity. He loved men but hated institutions. Sometimes, he would see it all so clearly that the sense of his own powerlessness would come.

He would cry, 'One man can't do anything. A man like me can't be heard—oh, I can't make myself heard! It is as if I were shut in a tomb.' He would only have been happy passing from one great crowd to another—harrowing, pleading, electrifying men. He would rise—even alone with me—to the heights of his power—and then fall into the valleys because no one could hear. That was his cry, *I can't make myself heard!* Then often, when he was waiting to speak, the power would come, and leave him drained when he faced his people. He would tell me afterward, 'If I could only have talked to them yesterday, or an hour before!'

"Then the doubt of self would come to him—the fear that he was wrong or insane. 'Berthe, it can't be that the crowds are wrong; that I am right—against all the crowds. It must be that I am insane.' He would suffer like one damned from that. Worse than all was the fear of his own Ego. He was more afraid of that than any other lion in the way. 'It isn't the cause, it's me—that wants to be heard. It's the accursed me that I am striving for—in agony to relieve. I merely use the Cause. All the time it is myself that I wish to make heard.' That would make him suicidal.

"I am only telling you these moods. He was a child, a play-mate, the loveliest companion a girl ever had—seeing the beauty and analogy in all nature and outdoors—full of jest and delights. I just wanted to show you the other side—"

It was all of breathless interest.

"There came a day," she added, as Peter watched her raptly, "when he did make himself heard, even as he dreamed...."

Peter thought of his reading the story—a boy at school, and was struck with the memory of its appeal to him in the light of the present.

"...The sustaining of his friends was taken from us at the last. They dared not come, of course. 'Berthe, little heart, it's all right,' he would say. 'You will have to go on alone, but the way will be shown you. You have the strength. You have been heaven and earth to me. I must go and leave you, but that's only a temporary matter. It will be hard—but it has been hard *with* me.... This is all right. It's good for what ails the world—but you are only a little girl! My God, I dare not think of it....'"

"I remember the dawn and the cold rain and the stone buildings—and then to find the world's relation to his daughter. That had been spared before. He kept it from me, and there was such a sustaining from his friends and power. Those most concerned are slowest to learn exactly what the world thinks of them.... It did not come until afterward, and then it almost killed me. I was clinging to a sorrow almost sacred, and I found that the world saw only the shame and madness of my plight. I suddenly saw it in the eyes of the people—how they drew apart from me.... He had only wanted to make them better. He said that all evil was the result of men hating one another. He did not hate men, but predatory institutions, false fatherlands, and all slave-drivers. They hanged him for that hatred, but what was more shocking was to find that the people whom he loved and served were horrified at his daughter...."

It did not detract from Peter's ardor that his intellect was away for an instant in a rather skeptical study of Metz Wyndham's life. To Peter had come glimpses of the magnificent selfishness of this prophet of the people. Did all great men have such an ego? If their lives were closely examined would they all reveal, in their intimate and familiar relations, the most subtle and insidious forms of self-service? In fact, was not the mighty *ego* the source of their record-making in the world? ... Peter banished this rush of conjectures.

Will Levington Comfort

Whatever the father, the whole art of the life of Metz Wyndham's daughter was the loss of the love of self.

"I feel before you," he said, "as I once felt in the vineyards beneath Vesuvius."

She smiled at him. "There are several ways to take that."

"Just one that I mean—and no explanation."

"... Peter, our last day together—all shadowy background to be put away—"

"And breakfast to occupy the immediate fore."

He went out into the street to purchase certain essentials, found some tall white flowers, and a copper vase to put them in. They were hungry, after the long night, and their happiness was the exquisite moments which they found between the darkenings. They would not permit the parting altogether to pervade. Her face was lustrous white; her eyes made him think of those gray days on the ocean, in which one can see great distances. More of a girl than ever she seemed to him, with her black hair combed loosely back and hanging in a pair of braids. The flowers stood tall between them.

"War weather like this makes one grow quickly," he said. "To think how easy and content we thought ourselves—even three days ago. Now, I want to say, 'Come, Berthe—come with me....' I want to take you to some quiet place, back in the States, in the country by the water. Yes, north country— by some lake that would be frozen when we got there. That's where the silence is, that winter silence. A cabin, a roaring fire—you and I together, alone. It seems you would be safe there, and I could begin to be satisfied—".

"Peter, Peter—don't make heavens to-day!"

"It's your particular heaven. No other would ever have made me think of *winter*—of something austere and silent for you to ignite."

"I wonder, shall it ever come to me—to have peace and abundance of nature? I have always had the cities, and now it is more war again—the opposite to nature—but I shall think every hour of that winter cabin. That is my place," she added. "Another would have made you think of the South—or the seas. I shall think of your being there with me—every day—no matter where I am—"

Her words had grown vague to his ears. Her lips were so red that for the time he saw them only. He arose and went to her around the tall flowers.

"What did you say?" he asked, after a moment.

"I don't know—oh, yes—perhaps, if we are very good in this war, and do all we can to make orderly our little circle of things in the great chaos—perhaps we may earn that winter cabin and the fireplace and the stillness. To plan our garden in the winter days—"

"I wish I hadn't spoken of it. It's almost unearthly far—in such a time. But, Berthe, will you ever be satisfied with one who hasn't the white fire of passion—as you have, in the cause of the peasants?"

"Oh, that's what I wanted to tell you. We are to be separated. We are grown up—a man and a woman. We dare speak to each other. At least, I dare.... Peter, I couldn't love you if you were all that—all that—" She hesitated.

"All that you missed in me last night?" he suggested.

"Yes, but I didn't miss it exactly. I was excited and overwrought. You are splendid with me. It is when others are near, that you are—cold and unemotional. I know it's your training—that thing you Americans have from the English. You are that way with men. You are not so with me. But, if you were like Fallows, or like my father, I could not love you. I would not dare—"

"Why?"

"First, I could not—and then I would not dare. First, that which we are, we do not love. We love another kind—for completion—"

"Clearly said. That must be true," he answered quickly. "And why would you not dare?"

"Because we should have a little baby, and it would suffer so in coming years. Peter, the poise and the balance—the very qualities I need in you, and which I love, the little baby would require as his gift from his father."

II

THE COURT OF EXECUTION

Chapter 1

"Hai, you, Peter—wake up!"

It was Boylan's voice, seemingly afar off, but coming closer.

"Wake up.... I say, young man, what do you think of it by this time?"

Thus Peter was awakened the seventh morning out—and in a place he had not observed the previous night. It was as good a place as usual, if not better, except for the smell of fish that had gone before. Clearly it had been a fish shop, business suspended some time. There were certain scaly trays on the sloping showboards to the street; scales glistened among the cobwebs of the low ceilings; also the floor was of turf, and doubtless very full of phosphor, an excellent base for rose-culture. The place dwindled and darkened to the rear, from which the head and shoulders of Samarc presently emerged, and a moment later Little Spenski, his companion, sat up and rubbed his eyes. These two, invariably together, were men of a rapid-fire battery, to meet their pieces lower in the fields,

Will Levington Comfort

and attached for the present, as were Boylan and Mowbray, to the staff of General Kohlvihr's command.

"Think of what?" Peter asked.

Boylan disdained answer. He was strapping a pigskin legging over a bulging calf, always a severe strain. He looked up presently, reached across and touched his fore-finger to Peter's chin then to his own, which bristled black and gray.

"Young man, you've got a secret," he remarked darkly.

Peter smiled. He kept his razors in the same case as his tooth-brush, and the case had not been mislaid so far. He could shave in the dark.

"You're either not of age, or your face is sterile," said Boylan.

"The floor of this fish shop isn't," said Peter.

"I've been with you the last forty-eight hours straight. No sign of life in that time."

"You went out looking for fresh meat at sundown. You were gone—"

"I was gone just five minutes, because the train wasn't up. You had tea on when I came back."

"There was a bit too much hot water."

"Peter, that will do once more, but I've got a suspicion. No man living can shave in the saddle—so you won't be able to spring that one. Besides, you are willing to discuss the matter."

"Did you ask what town this is?"

"No," said Boylan; "I couldn't remember if they told me. New town every night. The only thing to name a town is a battle. God, smell the wood smoke—doesn't it make you keen?"

"For what?"

Boylan looked at him. "What are we out for?"

"Apparently the column is out for blood, but I thought you might mean breakfast."

"The column will get blood, right enough," said Boylan, "whether it gets breakfast or not. What's the news, I wonder?"

"I've forgotten my relation to news.... Where are you going?"

"To see if that beef-train is in. I suppose you'll have rigged up a turkish bath and be in the cooling room by the time I get back."

Peter fed the horses and had tea and black bread served for two, by the time Boylan called from a distance: "Put on the griddle, Peter—a regular steak.... I stopped in the farrier's on the way back and had it anviled a bit. That's what kept me," he added.

Peter tossed it in the pan. Their fire was in the turf at the door of the fish shop. Boylan drew in close, having washed noisily, and deposited the remaining provisions in the two saddle-bags. "We're fixed for supper and breakfast," he remarked, with a sigh.

"You said that the army that would win this war must win through famine. The Russians had better begin—"

"I didn't say anything about Mr. B. B. Boylan—"

"Mr. Big Belt Boylan," Peter muttered, twisting his face away from the heat and sizzling smoke steam. The name held.

The huge Rhodes' man liked Peter more than the latter knew, and his likings of this sort were deep and peculiar. Boylan was nearing fifty, a man all in one piece—thick, ponderous, hard, scarred with *la viruela*, a saber sweep, a green-blue arc in his throat where some dart or arrow had torn its way in between vital columns. His head was bald and wrinkled, but very large, his neck and jaw to match, his eyes a soft blue that once had been his secret shame. Very often he had been called into the public glare.

"I was so hungry once," Boylan said, "that I've been a slave to the fear of it ever since." He referred to the Polar Failure. "Once in Farrel's Island—we were four," he added. "We drew lots to find out which one of us we must eat. That *was* a winter.... All you fellows may begin famine as soon as you like. You'll come a long way before you arrive at the personal familiarity of the subject earned by this same little fat boy.... Turn it again, Peter."

Samarc rushed past, speaking excitedly in French, and in the shadows behind they saw the eyes of Spenski, sympathetic and wistful.

"What did he say, Peter?" Boylan asked quickly. "Samarc's French is like my Russian."

"He said his face had been fixed for tea—and toast with Spenski—until we began to steam up the place. Now he's gone to the feed-wagons."

"Why, bless the ruffian, there's enough here for four."

"I told him that, but you know Samarc."

Little Spenski's voice now drawled from behind.

"We're getting low, anyway. It was right for him to fill the bags this morning, though very kind of you to offer—"

"I don't like that, Spenski," said Boylan. "Bull cheek for four was my order. Why, you fellows—"

Boylan was going to say how consistently generous with rations and private provisions the two Warsaw men had been, but got tangled in the language. Peter helped him. Boylan wouldn't have it otherwise, and quartered the steak, serving Spenski and covering the fourth with a tin. It was an excellent feast. For five days these two pair had cautiously, timidly even, stood for each other in that reserved way that much-weathered men integrate a memorable friendship.... Samarc returned. They helped him cache his provisions and drew him into the quadrangle around the fire. There was time for an extra pot of tea, and the dawn rose superbly. That day in the column Spenski was called into the personal escort of Kohlvihr, Boylan accompanying. Samarc and Peter rode as usual with the forward infantry—just behind the van, headquarters back a quarter of a mile.

"Tell me about Spenski," Peter asked. "He's an interesting chap. I heard him talking to you about the stars last evening, before supper, pointing out Venus and Jupiter."

"He'll grow on you," said Samarc, their talk in French. "He did in my case. We've been together six years in and out of the big instrument shop in Warsaw—Bloom's. We make a camera, microscopes and even a telescope now and then. I invented a rather profitable objective for the Blooms, for which they gave me a position, and a small interest that has kept me from wandering far from Warsaw. In the first days they told me about Spenski—his remarkable workmanship— and pointed out the wiry, red-headed little chap with the quick imperative smile you've seen. We got on well together from the first. It has been no small thing for me that he likes my ways. I got him in this service, by the way, and I don't know whether I'm very proud of that. He's a lot more famous as a workman now than six years ago."

"What is his work?" Peter asked.

"A lens-maker. His art is one of the finest of the human eye—requires genius to begin with. Spenski's craft on a glass in many cases doubles the price of the instrument. No one knows better what kind of a workman he is, nor can follow his particular finish with a keener or more appreciative eye, than old Dr. Abbe himself. Spenski has letters from that old master.

"He knows all sorts of out-of-the-way things—like the star stuff. He'll name for you scores of the vague, indefinite ones, not to speak of the larger magnitudes, which he can call by color at any hour of the night. It was this passion of his for the stars which showed him his work as a boy. That started him fabricating glasses to see them better. He has a supreme eye for light, circles and foci, and a brain that just plays with heavy mathematics—the most abstruse calculations. Yet, you see, he carries it all with the ease of a boy. I think men who come with a task to do are like that. It's part of them. They don't feel the weight of what they know, because it's all through them—not localized. You might be with Spenski an hour or a week and never know that he was more than just a mechanic—if you were just a mechanic."

"It's very interesting," said Peter, as charmed with his companion as with the man he talked about.

"A little while ago Spenski found his girl, and I would have withdrawn—for that is the high test," Samarc resumed. "But Spenski managed to keep us both without strain.... And then the war came along. A blight fell upon all workmanship in an hour. I had been on the military side of things from a boy, a matter of training and heredity. Of course, I would go. Spenski looked around the shop when I told him this. It was stricken, the machinery cranking down, the faces of the men white and troubled. 'I'll go, too,' said he.... I reminded him of her.... 'She wouldn't be interested in a chap who remained at home,' he said.... I told him of the big plants in Switzerland and America, where he could be of great value, but he was not tempted. 'I want to go if they'll take me in your battery,' was his last word on the matter.

"Of course I saw to that, but there's no work here, and there won't be, that can bring out Spenski's real values. Think of using such a man to feed the hopper of a rapid-fire piece.... But it's good to have him along. Spenski's a hard habit to break."

That night, when Boylan and Mowbray were together again, but a little apart from the others, Big Belt said:

"Say, Peter, that little Spenski is a card. A good little chap, smart and modest. I like him."

"I found Samarc worth cultivating, too," said Peter.

Chapter 2

Marching south along the Vistula with the old-fashioned army—no airships, nothing that intensely puzzled Mowbray in this service—that is, in the exteriors of it—nothing but earth poundage and earth power, a game that had much to do with earth and not with heaven. Seven quiet days of marching in splendid summer weather, the raw peasant soldiery well fed and comfortable, becoming a unit, all outbreak of separate consciousness anywhere more and more impossible, hardening to the peculiar day's work. They were used to heavy work, but this was a particular task that needed specific hardening of feet and lungs; also the personal idea in each breast required numbing. The physical aim was to make men light for heavy work; to give them a taste of the joy and the true health of the field—before the entrainments, the haste and the fighting; but the psychological purpose was to make each atom forget itself, to weave it well into the fabric of the mass. Kohlvihr's division had to be moved; very well, let the movement gather the values of practice marching as well.

A raw division, with a scattering of Poles and Finns mixed with the straight Slav peasantry and regarded by the Russian war office, as Peter Mowbray understood at once, a ticklish proposition. The cement for this new service was "green" as yet; it had to set, required frequent wettings of fine humor and affiliation. The marvel to Mowbray was that the thousands fell for it. They had practically all left something that was life and death to them—land, labor, women, children. Each had established the beginnings at least of a personal connection in the world, and this relation had to be rubbed out. What had they been promised to take its place? *Freedom*, doubtless. But intrinsically they were free men.

Peter recalled what Fallows had said: that properly fathered this peasantry might be led into a citizenship and virtue that would change the world. Instead they were to be impregnated with every crime. With such thoughts Peter felt the spirit of Berthe Wyndham awake in his mind.

Seven days and not a breath from the outer world. The correspondents were allowed to move in and out of Kohlvihr's headquarters; and, though they paid richly for everything, were treated well, and regarded as guests by the staff officers. Peter had met Kohlvihr in Warsaw before the thought of war—a good-tempered, if dull and bibulous old man, he had seemed in the midst of semi-civilian routine; but a different party here afield. Peter recalled the saying of old sailors that you never know a skipper until you ship under him.

Moments of evening, in the sharp hazes of wood smoke, when the whole army seemed nestling into itself, laughing, covering its nostalgia, putting on its strength, Peter met in certain moments the advisability of turning his back upon Boylan and Spenski and Samarc. The extraordinary nature of Berthe Wyndham would flood home to him, as to one to whom it belonged, very dear but very far.... He would smile when he thought of *The States* and the Old Man.... "He thinks I'm clutched in the ripping drama and waiting for blood," he muttered, "that I am burning to stop the breath of the outer world with my story of gore and conquest.... But I'm eating his bread. I won't betray. There must be a wise way to feed the red melodramatic receptivity of the cities and at the same time to tell the real story."

He stood in the midst of square miles of men and military engines. On every road other Russian forces moved southward and to the southeast. The railroads groaned with troops, for the most part in a better state of preparation than

Kohlvihr's division. Rumors reached the staff, as they neared the Galician border, that the Austrian fields below were already bleeding; finally word came, as they turned eastward, that they were to entrain at Fransic and make a junction with the main Russian columns preparing to invade Galicia from the northeast.

On the night before they entered Fransic, Mowbray awoke, and saw a figure sitting in the doorway of the little hut assigned them for quarters. It was Spenski, his face upturned in the starlight. He sat so still that Peter slipped out from the blankets (which covered Boylan as well) and took his place beside the lens-maker. Spenski was facing the east. The street of the little hill town lost itself in a sharp declivity just ahead; the nearer huts were low. The whole east was naked to the horizon and an indescribable glory of starlight.

"Aren't they amazing?" Spenski whispered. "It must be nearly morning, for those are the winter stars. I think they must have wakened me up. Do you know them?"

"Just the first magnitudes. They are more brilliant than I have ever known."

Orion and a great kite of suns stood out with new and flashing power.

"I never saw that huge *W* before—" said Peter.

"You don't mean Cassiopeia? Her chair isn't there, but over to the north—"

"No, no—*there*. Rigel, the upper right corner, down to the left, the Dog-star; up to Betelguese, down to the left again to Procyon, and up to the brightest of all—the stranger, not usually there—"

Spenski clutched him. "I was watching the bigger configuration, and didn't notice. Your stranger is the planet Saturn in transit between Taurus and Orion. Saturn completes the *W*, and the *W* stands for—"

"War, possibly," said Peter.

There was a growl just now from Boylan: "Come on back to bed, you star-gazers."

"Saturn is so far and moves so slowly," the little man whispered, "that the *W* will not be deranged for many months."

The hurry call for Kohlvihr came as expected in Fransic. The first sections of the divisions were entrained the next day— an end to summer road-work.... A day and night of intolerable slowness in a vile coach, and on the following noon the troop-train was halted, while a string of Red Cross cars drew up to a siding to give the soldiers the right of way; a momentary halt—the line of passing windows filled with cheering, weeping nurses.

Just one reposeful face—as both trains halted a second or two. It was the face of one who seemed to understand the whole sorry story, already to be contemplating the ruin ahead. Her hands were folded, the eyes intent upon the distance rather than the immediate faces of men. Mowbray could not articulate. Above all he wanted to meet her eyes, to put back the light of the present in them, but it was neither sound nor gesture that accomplished it; rather the storming intensity of anguish in his mind. His train jerked, her eyes found him, her arms raised toward him, lips parted. It became the one, above all, of the exquisite pictures in his consciousness, and the reality passed so quickly—gone, and no word between them.

Will Levington Comfort

Thus her colors came to him again—the mystic trinity of white and gray and black—all he had since known and loved added to the mystery of their first meeting. It was like an awakening to the rack of thirst after one has dreamed of a spring of gurgling water—the swift passing of that face of tender beauty and fortitude, that fair brow, gray eyes and black hair....

Boylan was looking deeply into his face.

"Good God, man, you're a ghost. What is it, Peter?"

"It struck me queer to see a trainload of girls down here in the field," said Peter quite steadily.

"Well, if a trainload of strange women can do that to you— here's hoping we never do Paris together."

Little Spenski opposite had seen the outstretched hands, and Peter saw that he had seen.

Chapter 3

And now a rainy field. Two days of cold wind and rain after the cattle-cars; a different tone and temper from the men, coughing instead of laughter at night-fall. Another nameless village—Galician, now, for the border had been crossed, and the stillest night Peter Mowbray had so far known among the troops. It was a listening army—the far distance breathing just the murmur of cannonading.

He moved about within the cordon of head-quarter sentries, studying the edges of the bivouac as the rain and the darkness fell. Kohlvihr's division was but a tooth of the main army now; the whole region was massed with Russians marching westward; but still the outfit from Warsaw was enough, all that he could encompass of the mystery of numbers. Others had met the enemy, but these were still virgin. They were listening.

Their faces looked white in the thickening dark, noses pinched and the rest *beard*.... Hair—it was like some rapidly ripening harvest in the command, different each day, making the faces harder and harder to memorize. Mowbray had been disgusted at first—faces like changelings, atrocious like chickens. But the beards were taking form now—all gradations of yellow and red and black—many of that gray-yellow which loses itself in the middle distance and becomes a blur. How he hated hair like that!

The next day dawned bright and cold. At ten Kohlvihr, in the midst of the southern wing, brushed the tail of an Austrian force in its turning. The engagement was sharp exhilaration to Peter; perhaps it was to certain of the soldiers; yet it was the first. Its touch of blood quivered through Kohlvihr's command not yet assimilated, stirred this raw entity with deep inexplicable passion.

The correspondents were riding with the staff; the point of the van was moving below in plain sight when its baptism fell. Kohlvihr licked his white lips, the upper lip uncontrollable like a deprived drunkard's. Below a skirmish was spreading out, the commands trumpeting back their messages. Mowbray turned. A little battery of mountain guns was racing forward through the infantry column, the drivers yelling for *gangway*. It was like a small town's fire department in action. Now the infantry poured down the rocky slopes that bordered the old iron road. Peter turned quite around in the saddle. The murmur in the air was queer—like something wrong below in a ship at sea. Kohlvihr's face interested him, the skirmish lines and their reinforcements, the voice of Boylan (though his faculties were too occupied to catch that rush of humorous comment in English); the mountain guns interested him, and the sudden racket of Russian riflery below.

Now one of the peasant soldiers was running up the slope from the van toward the staff. He was bare-headed, shocky-haired and bearded, making queer, high sounds like a squirrel as he ran—quite out of order and amazed at himself. He would have been struck down by his nearest neighbor ten days later, felled with the nearest officer's sword, but there was funk and a bit of dismay in the heart of the raw division that suffered the soldier to make his way to the staff.

Lifting his legs lumberingly, he held fast to his left wrist, where a bullet had started the blood. He held the wound high, like a trophy, the blood spurting, crying about it.... This was sudden discovery of something the army had started out to find, but had forgotten in the length of days. This was the red fleece—its drips of red were in each raw soul now. A little way farther and the staff awoke. An officer spoke. The peasant was caught and booted quiet. Kohlvihr licked his lips to keep them still. He perceived that Mowbray's eyes had fastened upon his mouth. The lips opened again. The order came forth for the soldier to be flogged.... It was their particular friend, Dabnitz, a lieutenant of the staff, who was given the execution of this order.

Chapter 4

The four were much together for a few days after that,
Samarc and Spenski not yet assigned to their battery. They
learned each other in those few days as men often fail to
learn the hearts of their immediate associates during years.
There was fighting—scattered, open, surprising often to one
out of touch with the points and the scouting. Different
towns every day, and a continual giving of territory on the
part of the Austrians.

"This is not the main fighting at all," said Boylan. "This is
but the edge of the game. It won't break into print. The big
stuff is farther on. These that we meet are the Austrian
columns hurrying forward. This territory is ours for the
marching through. We'll catch it later—and this will be
forgotten."

Samarc had known these towns that the Russian column was
passing through, yet he had to ask the names, because of the
destruction. The Austrians would always destroy in haste
before leaving, and more leisurely the Russians would
destroy. It seemed to affect Samarc, as some landmark
reopened from its ruin for his eyes,

"It seems to say," he told the lens-maker, "'I was this at one
time, and now I must go.'" Orders came for Samarc and
Spenski, but they were not to be remotely stationed, since
their battery was assigned to Kohlvihr's division—a different
camp but the same field. Few words about the separation, but
each of the four understood.... Night and day, the dead had
been with them in the recent days—in such richness and
variety they could not escape, could not cover them, and
something from the dead entered their hearts. To Peter—so
queerly were his thoughts running—the memorable incident

of their last night together had to do with an ant colony.

Supper was over, and they had tossed on a decayed log to keep up the fire. A nest of ants was presently driven forth by the heat from the soft heart of the wood. They found themselves hemmed in flame and turned back, as Peter thought, to seek the treacherous shelter of the nest again. It was not so; they were wiser than that, and marched forth in scores once more, each carrying an egg in its jaws. Spenski swung the end of the log out to the grass for them to make good their retiring. It was all very sane and admirable. Peter respected them....

The dead were with them. They had not learned to forget. Spenski would whimper in his sleep. The days did not fill him, wearied his body but other faculties and potencies were restless at night. This man who could grind a lens so that a line from the center of the earth to the center of the sun would pass through it without chromatic aberration, was more shocked than the other three by the cursory killing of the days, his imagination intoxicated and sleep perverted. His companion who imagined himself of coarser and heavier texture often placed his hand upon the dreaming one. Spenski would start, open his eyes and say, "Thanks, Samarc."

Continual rocking through the long days, and the rumbling of the earth from the artillery forward. A mountain country of sharply cool nights, of cool bright days—the scent of cedar and balsam, good water, steady skirmishing—food just a bit scarce so that the peasants snapped and bolted, showing sharp about the eyes. It was not hunger—just the lean kind of fare. Peter often watched the halted columns at night as the men sprang to the feeding. Supper fires burst forth at the drop of the rifles. Not so raw now, the Warsaw contingent, a military eye would remark—getting ripe, in fact.

A week afterward, Boylan reported at supper that they would be permitted to ride with the battery on the following day. In the meantime they had not seen nor heard of the other pair. Fighting and marching from dawn to nightfall usually; human nature refused effort after that. They were so near dead at night that they laughed about it, and felt their faces in embarrassment, sharp-boned and unfamiliar as the faces of the dead. Mowbray's was still clean shaven. Young Dabnitz, the exquisite of the staff, and a rather brilliant young Russian, was the only other who had kept his razors in order. Perhaps a woman ruled his heart, as Berthe Wyndham ruled Mowbray's.

Big Belt had lost his last reservation about his companion. He gave everything to Peter that he had given to Lonegan and something more—for the field called a little more, and perhaps Peter called a little more. The extent of Boylan's loyalty had nothing to do with words or matters of conduct so far, but it was a huge affair, a suggestion of which came to the younger man from time to time and humbled him.

Twice during the first fortnight, Boylan had asked if this were positively his first venture into the field with troops. "The reason I ask," he explained later, "is that you appear to have been on the job before."

This would have been a matter interesting to the Old Man of *The States*, according to Lonegan's story.

"I miss the little guy," said Boylan, referring to Spenski. They were anticipating the next day with the battery.

"I miss Samarc, too," said Peter.

Romanceless, remorseless routine. The day that followed was their hardest, for they were pressing the Austrians, taking their punishment but inflicting punishment, as if called of God to extinguish a nation. The face of the world seemed turned from them, in Peter's fancy. He marveled at what seemed the swift disintegration of an ancient worldly establishment like Austria—going down unsung. It was not like a country losing its identity, though that had to do with the facts; but rather like a shadow passing, to be followed, not by sunlight, but by another shadow of different contour and texture.

"We put such store by names," he muttered, as he watched the Austrian infantry give way before them, "and yet, the world will get on with other names just the same."

...There had been no chance for talk. They had merely pressed the hands of their friends, something darkly melancholy about Samarc, as if his eyes were in deep shadow, and something luminous in the eyes that shone from the haggard face of Little Spenski. They looked forward to the night, as men famished and athirst in a pit listen to the toil of rescuers. Almost the last thing that Peter remembered was that the moon came up before the sun had set. The rapid-fire battery was at work on a hot smoky hill, the shrapnel and larger pieces still higher, and the great masses of infantry moving below among the wind-driven hazes of the valley, their long necklaces, of white puffs, showing and vanishing.

Mowbray's ears were deadened to all sounds save from the immediate machine-guns and the big hounds above; to his eyes the swaying strings of infantry smoke-puffs in the valley were spectral and soundless.

The Russians had taken the little town of Judenbach in the early afternoon, but the Austrians gave them a stand two miles beyond, finding solid position in a range of craggy hills. The Russians had not cared to leave them there over

Will Levington Comfort

night, but the dislodgment proved difficult. The unlimbering of the batteries toward the end of the day on the shoulders of a thickly-wooded mass (from which Peter watched the infantry and the moonrise in daylight), was the final effort of the day to drive the enemy farther afield from Judenbach.

The two infantries were contending; gray Russian lines in the bottom land and already advancing up the slopes. Day after day, smitten and replenished—tillers of land becoming the dung of the land. Mowbray had always pitied the infantry, and watched them now with unspeakable awe and depression—moving up the slopes, lost in their white neck-laces of skirmish-fire, sprayed upon with steel vomit from the Austrian machines.

Samarc's battery was idle. It was often so, Boylan reported, when the enemy's duplicate pieces were busy.

Now withering—those gray Russian lines. They diminished, gave way, a thin ghostly pattern of the whole, falling back. An Austrian sortie of yellow-brown men to finish the task.

"That's *our* cue," Big Belt whispered.

The officers were already finding the range and fall. Samarc's machine was set, before his superior spoke. Peter saw what a week had done for him. Samarc seemed old at the task, already to have grown old. Spenski at the hopper— and the mutilating racket on. Between fire, Peter could not hold in mind the inconceivable magnitude and velocity of these sounds. His brain seemed to plow under, as it does the great events of pain, the impress of hideous suffering which the proximity of the machines caused. Yet at every firing the damnable things hurt him more. Fast beyond count, as the threads break in a strip of canvas torn with one movement— yet each crackling thread here meant projected steel.

They saw their work on the Austrian infantry lines. Yet always more infantry would come forth, and in the silence following the machines, the gray Russian lines stole forward again. Such was the slow battle vibration.

A company of sappers was below, opening the wood of the slope, so that the machine fire would not be impeded in case the Austrians drove back the infantry beyond the hollows at the bottom of the valley. A hundred yards down they were working like beavers among the trunks of cedar and balsam, when a shrapnel broke among them. The Russian higher batteries had been trying the same game among the Austrian emplacements, but could not see results.

All battery men near the two Americans knew well that the Austrians would note *that* explosion of their shrapnel, and would relate the range to the higher positions above. That one shot showed the Russian artillerymen that their position was untenable. It was not that the Austrians could see the damage they inflicted in one company of sappers, but that the shattering blow in plain sight from their position would show the exact means to displace the higher pieces that devastated their infantry.

"We've got to get out of here," Boylan whispered. Again as he spoke the orders to retire came quietly as a bit of garrison gossip, and as coldly. Horses came running down for the ammunition carts; every muscle of man and beast had its work now.

In thirty or forty seconds Austrian shrapnel would land higher. Peter was tallying off the seconds, wondering if they would get clear.... At this moment he noted that the moon had come up and that the sun was not yet sunk. The two on the eastern and western rims of the world were almost of a size and color, very huge and alike, except that one dazzled the eyes—the difference between incandescence and reflection. The whole dome was lost in florid haze. He almost laughed at what followed in his mind, so strange is the caravan of pictures that hurries through in action. It was the beauty above and ghastly waste of the infantry that brought back to his brain the reason and decency of the ants in the burning log—their order in contrast to this chaos....

The Austrians were workmen. Their searching shrapnel had been quite enough. Samarc's battery had begun to move, when they landed in the heart of it. All was changed about, and new. The silence was like a deep excavation, and the smell of fresh ground was in the air.

Peter did not see Boylan. He arose, half crawled up the torn ground to the place where Spenski and Samarc had stood. They were some distance—a saving distance for Mowbray—when he saw Samarc arise, his face sheeted in red. Samarc was staring about for Spenski. Presently, Peter followed the eyes of Samarc and saw the little man—half down, but looking up toward his friend, the eyes wide open; also Spenski's mouth, and the most extraordinary smile in the red beard.

Peter crawled a step nearer. There was no voice yet. He was tranced before this meeting of the companions, each of whom saw none but the other. Spenski had been partly kneeling, but as Samarc approached, his head bowed slowly down, and the smile was gone.

"Come on—they'll do it again!"

Peter heard the words—but did not know who spoke them—possibly Boylan from behind, possibly *he* had said it. He had not seen Samarc's lips move.

The voice was an offense in that silence.

Now Peter saw none but Spenski, until Samarc reached him, lifted, called. Peter saw the body raised from the ground to Samarc's arms—saw the little man's body open upon his friend like a melon that has rotted underneath.

Chapter 5

All went black for Peter. The slope rose up and took him. For an eternity afterward he felt someone tugging at him—hands of terrible strength that would not let him die, would not let him sleep. After that a familiar voice began calling at intervals.

"Hello," said Peter at last. "What have I been doing?"

"Not anything that you've pulled before. Is this an old habit?"

"What?"

"Passing out unhurt—lying like a log for an hour or two?"

"No, it's a new one. Where are we?"

"Judenbach. It's past supper time—"

Peter sat up, wobbled. The terrible hands steadied him again. He knew now what had lamed him.

"Where is she?" he asked.

"Huh?"

"I was wondering what hit me?"

"Now, you're getting glib again," said Boylan. Peter's reserve had interposed. His absence had something to do with her, but he could not remember. "Where is she?" had got away from him as he crossed the border back into the racking physical domain. He didn't like that.

"Did I say anything?"

"Nothing that will be used against you," Boylan observed. "As for what hit you—that's the mystery. Not a scratch in sight.... I was behind. You were standing still as a sentry after that shrapnel. Presently you bowled over—"

"That shrapnel?"

"Yep—"

There was an instant of silence; the picture returned and wrung a groan from Peter. All the energy of his life rebelled against *the fact*. Boylan's hand tightened upon him. For the moment Mowbray was in a kind of delirium.

"The moon had just come up," he said, "like another sun. The real sun was still in the sky from our hill."

"I know. I was there. Cut it, Peter."

"Where is Samarc?"

"In one of the hospital buildings, likely. I meant to find him as soon as I could leave you—"

"I'll go with you."

Big Belt fumbled in his saddled bags for a flask, brought it in one hand, a cup of water in the other....

They were in the streets, very dark. Once they were caught in a swift current of sheep driven in for the commissary. Judenbach sat on the slope of a hill, a little city, its heart of stone, very ancient, its "hoopskirts," as Boylan said, made of woven-cane huts. Already the stone buildings of the narrow main street were crowded with wounded. The correspondents were not permitted far either way from headquarters. Finally it was necessary to get Dabnitz of the staff to conduct them.... It had all been a jumble of ambulances at nightfall from the field, the lieutenant said. Russian soldiers were not ticketed. Many faces on the cots were bandaged beyond recognition. The three gave up at midnight, Peter gaining strength rather than losing it in the later hours. Orders were that the streets be emptied of all but sentries.

"No, nothing like that—" said Boylan, as Mowbray sank to the floor by his blanket roll. "You haven't had supper—"

"Don't, Boylan.... I say, what do they do with the dead?"

Rain was pattering down; the smell of drugs reached them.

"It *does* make a difference when you know one of them— doesn't it?.... God, man, we're cluttered with wounded. The dead are at peace—"

"I wonder what stars he's watching to-night?"

"Come, come. Peter—"

"I know.... I know, Boylan. Only it shows me something. He was a great workman. There are things in the world that can't be done because he's gone. There are others like him. He had a girl. He had a friend. He had us—"

Boylan decided that talking was good. He listened and prepared soup.

"And to-morrow they're at it again," said Peter.

"It won't look the same in the morning—"

Peter did not answer.

"Anyway, you didn't bring on the war, Peter—"

"It makes a man cold with that kind of cold a supper-fire don't help."

"Peter, you've got me stopped with your moods—like a woman. Women were always too profound for Mr. B. B. Boylan—"

"Sorry. You've been a prince. I'll do better now. I'll get out of it. Little shock—that's all. I think it wasn't so much physical. Something changed all around. I've been taking things as I found them so long. That helps to bring on a war—"

Boylan glanced at him narrowly.

Peter laughed. "I'm all right. Head's working."

Big Belt sighed. "I loved that little guy, too. God, I'd run east to Asia and keep on running rather than meet his girl."

Peter drank hot soup and slept. Next morning it was like a hard problem that one has slept upon and awakened with the process and answer straight-going. They had not searched ten minutes (calling "Samarc" softly among the cots where the faces were bandaged) before a hand came up to them. It was Peter who took it; and as their hands met, the whole fabric of the man on the cot broke into trembling. They understood. Samarc had been lying there rigid with his tragedy. Peter's touch had been enough to break the dam of his misery.

"*I have ceased to kill,*" he said.

The head was twice as big with bandages; yet under that effigy, so terrible was the intensity of the moment, Peter became conscious of ruin there, also of a sudden icy cold in the morning air. Samarc's powerful hand still clutched his. The voice that had emerged from under the cloths was still in his ears. It had seemed to come as water from a pipe—loosely, the faucet gone. The hand was unhurt.

"...He came in the night. I did not speak—but my heart was fighting against the guns. He was moving here and there. He turned to me, as if I had suddenly cried out, 'What shall I do?'...'You can cease to kill,' he said."

Boylan was watching Peter. His face turned gray.

They received the intelligence of the words, as they came, although at another time the mouthing would have been inarticulate as wind in one of Judenbach's archaic street-lamps.

"I'll stay with him, Boylan," said Peter, choosing the hardest thing, but Big Belt would not leave, though the Russian columns were moving in the street—off to renew the battle among the hills. The two sat by until Samarc slept.

* * *

They were in the street again, moving close to the walls, for the cavalry was crowding the narrow highway. They crossed finally to a stone-paved area at the side of Judenbach's main building. Their feet were upon the stone flags of this court, when Dabnitz suddenly hurried forward, with a gesture for them to stand back.

"Just a moment, my friends," he said. "A little formality, but very necessary—"

Peter lifted his eyes, perceived three men standing bare-headed against the wall of head-quarters, twenty paces away. One of them exclaimed, his voice calm but penetrating:

"We are not spies. We do not care to turn our backs. We are not afraid to die, for we have made our lives count—"

It was the voice of a public speaker; the voice of a man making good many words.... Dabnitz stepped between Boylan and Mowbray, stretching out his arms before them. It was all in an instant. They saw Dabnitz's apologetic smile—and a Russian platoon at their right, rifles raised—then the ragged volley.

Each of the three fell differently.

Chapter 6

Boylan and Peter sat together in the ante-room of headquarters. They did not speak. Peter was getting down to the
quick. He thought many things which a man never tells
another man, and seldom tells a woman; yet they were
matters of truth and reason, no sentiment about them. He
recalled many incidents of early years in which his mother
had tried to teach him sensitiveness and mercy. Until now
her effort seemed to have been wasted. It had been more
simple and appealing to him to follow his father's picture of
manhood. Possibly his mother had wearied of pitting her will
against his. He had grown up under his father's control and
ideal. As it looked to him now, he had become all that was
obvious and average and easy; while his mother's passion
had been for him to become one of the singular and precious
and elect.... He would never have seen this so clearly had it
not been for Berthe Wyndham. She had given him a kind of
new birth, taken up the work wherein his mother had
failed....

Dabnitz came in. The young staff-officer was handsome,
soldierly, black-eyed. His manner was one of enfolding
cheerfulness. He had proved fair and kindly, temperate in his
tastes and delicate in his appreciations of humor and natural
effects. He could express himself fluently in Russian,
German, English and French, but was a caste-man to the
core, a militarist and autocrat. As such he proved rather
appalling to Peter Mowbray on this day.

"Is General Kohlvihr out with the fronts?" Boylan asked.

"He's in the field, but not at the front. We got the point
yesterday, you see. I'd rather be in the van every day than left
to these matters of clean-up—"

Peter looked up at him. "Is there much of this to do?"

"I'm afraid so. They work among the hospitals. You don't catch many of them in the ranks—"

"Perhaps they would rather tend the wounded than to make the wounds."

Dabnitz smiled cheerfully. "They're afraid of their hides. When a man does a lot of talking, he is generally shy on action—"

Peter saw the ease of the acceptance of this view on the part of the others; saw how clearly it was the view of the military man.

"And yet it was a clean-cut death of that talker and his two companions you just executed—"

"An exception now and then," Dabnitz granted.

"How do you catch them?"

"We have a system at work for that purpose—everywhere, especially in the hospitals. There isn't much temporizing when we get them."

Peter Mowbray's skull prickled with heat and his face was cold with sweat.

"What do they preach?" he managed to ask.

"Sometimes for men to rise and go home; sometimes for them to cease to kill, and sometimes to shoot down the officers. It isn't all that a man has to do now to lead his men forward," Dabnitz observed. "He must do that, of course, but all the danger isn't in front. It doesn't follow that a man has turned his back upon the enemy nowadays—if he happens to be found with a wound in the back."

"Were these—these that you put out this morning—working in the hospitals?"

"Yes."

Peter turned away.

"In a good many cases we bring a man to his feet again from a bad wound—to find him not a soldier but a damned anarchist."

"It's expensive and cumbersome also to carry such a hospital system afield," Peter observed.

Dabnitz did not catch the irony. "Yes, it would be cheaper and simpler to put a hard-hit soldier out of his misery—"

Boylan, watching Peter's face, suddenly arose, suggesting that they ride out toward the fighting. ....When they were alone, he added:

"I know you don't want the front to-day, but it was very clear that I'd better get you out of there....Peter, did you ever kill a man?"

"No." The question did not seem wild to either of them— there by the open court of Judenbach.

"I knew a man who did. I saw him getting whiter and whiter like your face—and looking into his victim's eyes in that queer surprised way you looked at Dabnitz. It wasn't in the field; in a city bar-room. I didn't look for what happened—

but I knew something was coming. The fool went on talking, talking. The other watched him, and when all the blood was burned out of him....Great God, here I am talking blood—"

"It's in the air," said Peter. "It's hard to breathe!....No, I won't go down front to-day. I wish I could go back—back—oh, to the clean Pole—no, to some little snowy woods in the States....Boylan, does it suffocate you?"

"It's different from anything I knew," said Boylan. "It's so damned businesslike. Something's come over the world. War was more like a picnic before. I never saw it like this. I believe we've gone crazy."

They stood before the main building, just at the entrance of the stone court—halted by the hideous outcry that reached them from another building just a few doors below. It was as if a strong man were being murdered by torture. The big cannons boomed up the narrow cobble-paved road from the field. As far as they could see in either direction, the street was crowded with soldiers, stepping aside for artillery going south, and the stream of ambulances coming in from the front. Passing them now from the street into the court was a cortege, little but grim—a Cossack trooper leading two bare-headed men by a rope attached to his saddle, a Cossack non-commissioned officer walking behind with raised pistol. Both the prisoners were young, one a mere boy, yet he was supporting the elder. Peter's eyes turned to the blank wall of the main building where Dabnitz had been busy as they passed. To the right, in the gloom from the walls, was a row of iron gratings, the windows knocked out—darkness under the low stone lintels.

Peter had not noticed before this dim square, within the square. His mind dwelt upon it now in the peculiar way of the faculties, when thoughts are too swift and too terrible to

Will Levington Comfort

bear....It was like something he had seen before, the dark little square. Yes, it was like part of a recess yard he had known in an old school-building years ago....

He couldn't keep off the reality long. In every direction the murderous army—no song, no laugh, no human nature, no love, no work, but death. He was imprisoned. And some-where near or far in the midst of such a chaos, was Berthe Wyndham. Could she live in this?.... Peter was suicidal, very close to that, a new thing to him. Queerly he realized that death would be easy for himself, simple, acceptable. For there was no escape. They would not let him go. There was no place that one could go out of the army. Not even the dead go back.... It would not be fair to her. She might live, and call to him afterward. He did not think she could live, but there was that chance. He thought of his mother—quite as a little boy would, his lip quivering.... He started at the touch of Boylan's hand.

"I'll tell you what we'll do," Big Belt said. "We'll write, Peter. We'll get out the machines to-day. We'll write a story—just as if we could file it on a free cable. It will do us good. We'll tell the story—"

"We'd have to eat it....Boylan, if I should tell this story on paper, the Russians would burn it and me and the house in which it was written....No. I must work better than that. Come back. I want Dabnitz—"

Boylan drew him face about.

"You're not going to—"

"No—no. I wasn't thinking of killing him. It wouldn't do any good. One would have to kill all the officers and save enough energy for the Little Father at the last. No, I want him to help me—"

They found him at headquarters.

"Lieutenant Dabnitz," Peter said, his hand upon the Russian's shoulder, speaking very quietly, "I feel like a fool doing nothing all day long—and so much to do. I want you to take me over to that hospital Samarc is in, and set me officially to work. Let me be orderly, anything, to-day. I want to help, if you'll forgive me—"

"Gladly, Mr. Mowbray. I'm sure they'll be very glad. Of course, they are always short-handed in the hospitals."

"Thanks."

Boylan's heart gave a thump at the new light in Mowbray's eyes.

"I'll go along, too," he said. "I'm the daddy of them all, when it comes to lifting."

A ragged platoon volley crashed from the court as they entered the street. Peter's steps quickened.

Chapter 7

Of course, they did not know it in *The States'* office, neither the Old Man nor his managing editor, but a way had been found to *rock* Peter Mowbray. Indeed he would have been rocked to pieces had he not found his work that day in Judenbach. ....When no one was listening, he would talk to the wounded. Peter discovered that there was a woman in him, as many a field-man has discovered. In fact he came to believe that we are all mixed men and women, and that it is the woman in us that suffers most. He had a suspicion that there was a woman in Boylan, and had to smile just there. He sank into the work, and saved himself. Samarc appeared to be asleep.

He would have laughed to have heard his own talk afterward. A man does not remember what he says to a loved horse, or to a dog that looks up in passing. Innocent as that, Peter's sayings to the wounded and dying. Had there been spies about, the American would have been counted eminently safe. He had to talk; his heart was so full; it was part of the action that saved him. All the time there was in the background of his mind a steady amazement at himself— something of his, aloof, watchful, that was not exactly ready to accede to all this change and emotion, and yet was not strong enough to prevent.

Twice through the long forenoon he saw a little black-whiskered orderly, eyes dark and wide and deep, his nose sensitive and finely shaped, his shoulders unsoldierly. Once his cap fell as he went to lift a pan, and Peter saw as noble a brow as ever dignified a man. He went to him and, as he stood there, he found there was nothing to say.

"Who are you?" the other asked.

"That's what I was trying to think to ask you?" Peter said with a smile. "I am Mowbray, an American correspondent—"

"Why are you here?" He pointed to the cots.

"I had to do something."

"The misery called to you?"

"Perhaps. To be sure, I'd better say my own misery made me come."

They talked in French.

"It is all the same. You are not a beast."

"I'm not sure," said Peter.

"That is good, too. I'm glad you have come. All morning I have watched you...."

"You did not answer me. Who are you?"

"I am Moritz Abel."

He held a wash basin in one hand, a bit of linen in the other—this man who had done such a poem that the glory of the future flashed back through it, to sustain and to be held by men. It was a queer moment. Facing each other, Mowbray thought of Spenski—as if the little lens-maker stood behind the narrow shoulders of the poet.... Was it only the little red-headed body that they had killed"? Would the immortal come back with a new story of the stars? Thus Peter found himself thinking of Spenski, with this lover of new Russia before him. And would the destroyers slay this one too?...

Now his humanity came back in a cloud, and he shuddered at the thought of Russia murdering the man who wrote *We Are Free*.... Perhaps it was the woman in him that made him say:

"I hope *you* live through the long night, Monsieur."

Moritz Abel stepped nearer. In the silence Peter grew embarrassed. What he had said would sound without footing since the poet did not understand the trend of his thoughts. He meant to, add what *the long night* signified, and wanted his saying really known for what it was—an utterance of pure passion against the destruction of genius. The other replied, making all explanation unnecessary:

"I knew you for one of us. It is the long night, but it is a great honor for us to be here and at work."

"Where are your companions?"

The Russian smiled. "They are all about through the dark of the long night. We may only signal in passing. In fact, I must go now—"

The surgeon in charge had entered. Peter went to Samarc's cot, steeling himself. "Samarc," he whispered, without bending, "Samarc—"

The wounded man stirred a little, moaned, but did not answer.... In the far corner Boylan was moving cots (occupants and all) closer together for the admission of more. His sleeves were rolled. Near him a little woman, whose waist was no larger than the white revelation of Boylan's forearm, was directing the way, the giant of the Polar Failure struggling to please. Something of ease and uplift had come to Peter from this, and from the passing of Moritz Abel. Silently battling with Dabnitz, with Kohlvihr, with king's desire and the animal of men, was this service-thing greater than all, greater than death.... A soldier called and he went toward the voice. Presently Peter was jockeying him into good humor with low talk.

All day the battle tortured the southern distance—the canno-nading nearer, as the hours waned. The Austrians were holding their own or better. It was the fiercest resistance which the Russian columns had as yet encountered. All afternoon wounded were brought back. It became more and more difficult to move among the cots in the building. So it was with all Judenbach that was not in ruins. Twice through the afternoon there were volleys in the court below; and when the two went forth for food, they saw a soldier carrying baskets of dirt from the street, and covering the stone flags close to the main building.... And from that grim house a little down the street, came at intervals, shocking their senses, the hideous outcry as of murder taking place.... Boylan went down into the field an hour before sunset, Peter back to the hospital.

"I'll see what I can find," Big Belt remarked. "You're right to go back, Peter. As for me, I can stand it better outdoors."

Crossing the street, it seemed to Peter that he had been in Judenbach certain ages, a reckonable space of eternity—despite the lowering sun which calmly informed him that at this time yesterday the Austrians had found the range of Samarc's battery with a shrapnel or two. Many things had come to him. He wished as never before for a free cable.... Boylan came in at dark and drew him away from Samarc's cot.

"I'll be back to-night," Peter promised.

"...There's been no break in the check to-day," Big Belt reported. "Kohlvihr's division, and the immediate forces surrounding, are part of the great right wing, and this right is holding up the whole Russian command. I heard Kohlvihr explaining to the Commander's aide that the Austrians here had been reinforced; that they gave us Judenbach for the taking yesterday, in order to fall back into the hills beyond. The center and left, it appears, is clear, ready to fight on to Berlin or Budapest, but the whole line is held up for this right wing. Kohlvihr is desperate. There'll be a hard pull to get across the hills to-morrow—all hands, Peter."

"This may be our last night in Judenbach then?"

"If killing a division will start a hole across that range of hills, it's our last night—"

I'll sit it out with Samarc," Peter said.

"Go to it, if you think best. You were a mighty sick woman this morning. Something in yonder helped you. I'll see you through for another treatment."

"Boylan, don't you stay up. You've roughed it to-day and been afield. Don't let me spoil your sleep—with a big day ahead. It wasn't lack of sleep that got my nerve this morning—"

"Oh, I'll yap around till bedtime," said the other. "What does Samarc say?"

"Something has come over him. Some one came to him last night and seemed to drive a nail right into his thinking—pinned him."

"He's turned against the killing?"

"Yes. And he'll be restless to-night, sleeping so much to-day.... At least, he made the appearance of sleeping. I think he was shocked to hear his voice.... His eyes are right enough. But below—"

"What made you think he had the appearance of sleeping?"

"It just occurred to me. He didn't want to take all my time. I whispered his name several times—no answer. Once when I was leaving, his hand reached up and touched my coat."

"Is he hurt badly?"

"Not a thing in the body. It's between his throat and his eyes.... You know I saw him last night after the shrapnel as he lifted—it was just a sheet of blood. Afterward it was covered in cloth. I don't think he knew until this morning, when he started to talk."

"He was all knit to the little man," Boylan said. "As good a pair as I ever met afield.... Oh, I say, eat something—"

Peter smiled at the big fellow and turned to his soup and black bread. He didn't say what he thought, but it had to do with his own field companion this time.

* * *

...Midnight. Boylan had gone back to quarters. Peter's ward was low-lit and still. ...The wounded man's hands waved before his bandage, as if to detract attention from the windy blur of his utterance. Samarc wanted to die.

"You know it was because of me that he came—" he repeated.

"But you mustn't suffer for that. Really, Samarc, a man couldn't have been a better friend than you. Spenski would tell you so if he could. These are times for men to *live*. I wanted to kill myself this morning. You know I was behind you on the hill, too. That, and the tragedy all about, and then they were murdering spies and martyring real Fatherland men out in the court—as if there wasn't enough death afield. It was too much for me. Old Boylan helped me, but if I hadn't come in to work, I'd have shot my head off. Here— men dying hard and easy; men and women serving; so much to do,—I got better. Death isn't everything. I'm not a genius or a dreamer, man. I'm so slow at dreaming and brotherhood and all that, that a woman once ran from me. But I saw to-day that death isn't all. I don't know what else there is, but this is a sort of long night, this war. A few of us are awake. If we are put to sleep—that's all right—I mean knocked out, you know. But so long as we are not, we've got to watch and root for the dawn. God, man, there is much to do. We've got to make our lives count—"

He was bending forward talking very low. He thought from the pressure of Samarc's hands that he was gaining ground. It was queer and laughable to himself—this line of talk that came to him. He knew so well the pangs of that suicidal suffocation, that he could talk for the very life of the other. He added:

"A little black-whispered man looked up from his soap and towels this morning. His hat fell off, and I saw he had come a long ways. He looked at me again, and I spoke to him. Samarc, it was another of these little whirlwinds of human force—a master workman like the man you loved.

"It was Moritz Abel who wrote *We Are Free*....

"And there are others—like Spenski and Abel—some of them dead—some to die to-morrow. Do you think the good God would let them die so easily if it wasn't all right? But we mustn't die without making our lives count."

Peter's eyes were covered by slender hands. It was like passing a garden of mignonette in the night, that fleeting perfume of the hands.

"Oh, Peter, how sweet to see you and hear your voice!"

It seemed that he became molten in her presence. A heavenly *adagio* after a prolonged movement of sin and shame and every dissonance. It was as if she had come from a bath of peace to him; another inimitable moment in the life of his romance. He turned to her, holding fast to the hand that was stretched toward him. He cleared his voice.

"Excuse me, Samarc," he said.

III

THE HOUSE OF AMPUTATIONS

Chapter 1

They looked long into each other's faces. "You were wonderful as you spoke of your friend. Did you know that, Peter?"

He turned away deprecatingly.

"Forgive me. Of course you didn't know." "...And you meant to come all the time?" he asked at last.

"Yes."

"I should have known it.... That day—that day across the siding—why, Berthe, it was almost more than I could stand. I had just been thinking of you."

"We were like two spirits who hadn't earned the right to be together," she said.

"I'm afraid it's dangerous now," he answered. "One mustn't have a whim, other than to extinguish the enemy. The army is afraid of itself. All day—"

Will Levington Comfort

Though he checked himself, she knew his thought.

"Yes, all day, they murdered white-browed men in the court below."

"Berthe—"

"Yes."

"I want you to guard your life—as if it were mine—just that."

All surroundings were melting away from them. She had never seen him like this.... Even Samarc could not hear their whispers.

"You came like an angel, Berthe,—all I ever want of an angel. I tell you I am proud."

"Of what, Peter?"

"That I had sense enough to go a second time to the Square at Warsaw."

"I'm glad, too.... If we were only in the winter stillness—"

They were silent. Samarc's hand came up to Peter, and drew him close. It was clear that he could not bear the woman to hear his struggle for speech. "Tell her about Spenski," came to Peter's ears in the lipless mouthing.

Berthe saw that Peter was ghostly white, as he lifted his head. She thought it had to do with what the wounded man said.

Peter began at random, gathering his thoughts on the wing.

Nothing hurt him in quite the same way as that suggested havoc under the bandage. He steadied himself, and talked of the little lens-maker. Strength came from the joy he was giving Samarc.... It seemed that they were quite alone. He told of the night of stars, of the little man's superb sensitiveness.... She bent to Samarc at last.

"You wanted him to tell me?"

He nodded. There was something intensely pathetic in it all. Her eyes were full of light.

"The story thrills me," she whispered. "Oh, this is very far from a hopeless world. What I have seen to-day—even the fortitude of infamous men—manhood, black and white—the war within the war. Don't you see, all Russia is out here in the wilderness casting forth her demon? We must not mind blood nor death—for the result means the life or death of the world's soul!"

Once she would have seemed very far and remotely high to Peter Mowbray.... They had drawn a little apart from the cot.

"What made you so white?" she asked.

"It's my weakness. We rode together for days and quartered together. He was so clean-cut. It's the way his words come. And he seems so utterly bereft without the little man."

She pressed his hand in understanding.

"Berthe, do you sleep? Do you take food? Are you well? Are they good to you? Can you live through?"

"Yes, and what of you?"

"All is quite well with me. I can endure anything with the hope of taking you home afterward."

"We must be ready to give up that, too. It is hard; it's our ordeal—but if the end should appear, we must find strength to look it in the face. These are the times for heroics. Every real emotion that I have ever known is a lie—if those who love each other well enough to love the world—do not pass on. Why, Peter, you said the same to him—speaking of his friend and Moritz Abel, 'Do you think the good God would let such men die so easily, if it weren't all right?'"

"Did I say that?"

She drew back her head, looking him through and through.

"Peter, it's the child in you that I love. You're so much a man, and they all think of you as a man, man—all your training to be a man—and yet it's the child that a woman's heart sees and wants to preserve for her own."

"Do you see much of Moritz Abel?" he asked.

"Yes.... It was he who found you for me."

Peter was watching her red lips now. It was like that morning in her room, the tall flowers between. He did not hear what she was saying. The room was dim. Samarc's face was turned from them. One man in a near cot flung his arms about his head wearily, but his eyes were toward the wall.... He caught her in his arms and loved the beauty of earth in her face.

"...Peter, we must forget ourselves!"

"I can't forget you. I want you as you are," he repeated in

tumult. "I want you here in the world—as you are now! We'll stand for what we can't help. There's no use fighting the end if it comes. The greatest thing here to a man will be the greatest thing after he's dead—that's clear enough. But I haven't had you here—only a few minutes. I want the winter stillness *on earth*—in the woods—not in some paradise yet."

"Hush—I want it too. Oh, you can never know how much!... I had better go now—"

"Not until I know all about you. To-morrow is to be the big day of the battle. All may be changed. If it's a Russian victory, this is our last night in Judenbach—"

"You will go out to the fronts?"

"Yes, for a little, but I shall watch how the day fares, so I can hurry back."

"To-day—we were just a stone's throw apart. I was in that building down the street—the amputation cases."

"Not the house where those cries come from?"

"Yes, we work there. Moritz Abel, Fallows, Poltneck, the singer, and others.... This morning I thought I could not bear to live. It was as you told him—about yourself. You see we had no anesthesia, except for cases of life or death—among the officers."

"And you came to me from a day like that?" he asked unsteadily, his passion blurred, even the beauty of it. The chance of her living had suddenly darkened.

"It was like coming home," she whispered. "...In Warsaw before your day—sometimes crossing the Square in the darkness—I used to think what it would mean to come to a house of happiness, after a long cruel day. It seemed too far from me; sometimes even farther than now. When I came in here to-night, and heard your voice—I knew what it would mean to come home. We must not ask too much. Many have never known what has been given to us—in these few minutes."

"We must not ask too much," he repeated.

She saw that he had a vivid picture of her day in that house of amputations, that the picture had stunned him.

"But, Peter, I have seen such courage to-day. It was a revelation. All that I had seen of isolated courage before in the world—all was there to-day, and ten times more, there in the blood and torture. And Poltneck sang to them—sang to the maimed and limbless—sang through the probings—with the sound of the cannon in the distance and more wounded coming in. He sang of home and Fatherland—even of the old Fatherland. The many love the old still; it is only the few who love the dream of the new.... We must not ask too much. The new spirit is being born into the world. This war is greater than we dream of. In Warsaw I could see only the evil, but here—under everything—is the humble and the heroic in man. Hate and soldiery are just the surface. That which is beneath will be above—"

She was far from him now; the white flame in her face. He saw that he could only go on through the days and work and wait and trust in the God he had told Samarc to trust in. How easily—without an impress of memory, he had said that; and how heroic to accomplish—for mere man.

He did not answer—just looked at her. He saw her turn and smile. Moritz Abel was standing there.

"I cannot tell you—what it meant to me to see you two standing so," he said. "And this place of quiet—you two and your paradise!... Let me see, it occurred to me to suggest—"

He found himself reluctant to finish. He had spoken lightly as if to propose that they would be more comfortable in another room—but his thoughts concerned the volleys in the court. They knew it.

"The staff knows me rather well," said Mowbray. "I was counting on that, but one cannot be sure—"

"There has been no secret," she said. "Will you come in the morning before the columns go out?"

"Yes, it will be early."

"I'll be watching. If not—he will be there to tell you why."

Peter turned to the poet. "Watch over her—won't you?"

"You honor me, Mr. Mowbray. All that I can do—be very sure of."

She went to Samarc's cot and took his hand. Peter saw her face differently, as she leaned. It was one of the mysteries that her tenderness was the face of one woman, her sorrow another.

"Good-by—good-night."

.... A little later Peter found himself with Samarc's hand in his. He had been sitting by the cot watching the war within the war, head bowed on his free hand. It was a struggle of white and black—of knights and kings, plumes and horses, white and black.... Now the wounded man seemed sending

Will Levington Comfort

messages through his hand. The lamps were low.

"It's been the day of days, Samarc," Mowbray said. "You brought me something that I needed very much. I wish I could do as much for you. Let me know, won't you, if I can?... Yes, I'll be right here through the night—"

He heard the tread of soldiers in the hollow-sounding court below—clanking accouterments, heavy steps. There was a halt, a voice, and a long moment before he breathed. It was just a change of sentries, perhaps.

Chapter 2

Just a moment's talk in the street—twice interrupted by sentries, as they moved the hundred yards from the courtyard of Judenbach to the house of amputations.

"...He was trying to lift a man from the hopelessness of death when I stepped up quietly behind," Berthe was saying. "He was wonderful about it, because he had felt the same hopelessness. I wish you could have heard him."

Moritz Abel said: "He is effective. He is intellect and heart— very sound. His vision will come quickly. He does not wing—that is our trouble. We are carried away. He is still within the comprehension of the average man. We need him greatly. Also he needs us. What a man he would be to steady us—to interpret for us. The new Fatherland must have such men. It has been our destiny always to dream and to pass— another generation to make our vision flesh—"

"You mean such men as Peter Mowbray would be direct interpreters?" she asked.

"Exactly. We are poets and artists and singers. We are the fathers of the new Fatherland in a sense, but we need among us lawgivers and statesmen—men who love men straight and not through the arts—men who have the same zeal for men that the arts give us when we are pure, but who are conservers and constructors, men of great force and acumen and kindness—"

"Oh, I know so well what you mean," she whispered. "If you could only have heard him with the bandaged man—*'I am not a genius or a dreamer, man. I am so slow at dreaming and brotherhood, and all that, that a woman once ran away*

Will Levington Comfort

from me. But I saw to-day that death isn't all.'"

"Yes, that is it," Moritz Abel said. "That is the quality. And many times among those who do not make claim nor talk of brotherhood, the reality is beaming from their daily service. Yes, that is it. I hope to know him better after the long night."

They had reached the place of blood and torture.

"And now you must rest a little," he told her. "You know he asked me to take care of you. I like him for that. A man would see a great deal in that, for he honored me."

"And me—" she whispered.

Chapter 3

It was not yet dawn. Peter heard the moaning of the men as they awoke and turned in their bandages. Surgeon and assistants passed through; two of the latter remained to start up the malingerers. Machine and rapid-fire men especially were needed at the front, it was said. Four thousand men had fallen in the past three days, and this was to be the day of the most furious battle—Kohlvihr to drive a hole through the hills, this day. An early incident revealed certain facts—personal—and had a temporary numbing influence upon Mowbray. The day had risen and Samarc awakened, when a strange orderly entered the ward, and came leisurely to the cot where Peter sat:

"What have you here?"

"A shrapnel wound in the face."

The orderly looked under the cot for the uniform, as if to determine Samarc's place and rank.

"Where's the blouse?" he asked.

"It was covered with blood," said Peter. "They took it away."

"What branch of the service?"

Peter was not sure—infantry possibly. He didn't care for the stranger's manner, nor to have this particular gunner of the rapid-fire pieces hurried to the field unhealed. The orderly bent suddenly, whispering.

"She told me to tell you that she wants to come, but that it isn't safe—"

...Moritz Abel looking for an interpreter would have been interested now; also the Old Man of *The States*. The stranger had spoken leisurely. Peter's temptation was conquered before he was half through.

"Are you sure you were to give me some message?" he asked.

"Yes."

"But I wasn't expecting anyone."

The other regarded him keenly. Peter was well trained for that. An officer appeared in the doorway and beckoned the orderly.

"It must have been a mistake," the latter muttered.

Peter was thinking fast. The fact remained that their meeting the night before had been noted. He was leaving for the field shortly; the harm of suspicion would fall upon her.

"I promised to call a moment this morning at the amputation house—but no one was to come for me," he added.

"I have made a mistake," the orderly repeated.

"...I wonder if I have?" Peter thought.

Samarc's hand came up to him, and the pull that meant he wanted to speak. Peter invariably paled before this ordeal. Not through words but sounds were the meanings tortured out.... Samarc meant to take the field. In the usual course there would be no coming back for him at nightfall, because he had "ceased to kill—"

"But must your officers know?" Peter whispered.

...The officers would know if it were the same old crew, because they knew Samarc's work. This was the substance of the answer.

"But why go?"

...They would take off the bandages to be sure that he required further hospital care. He could not endure that. The bandages must never come off.... He would rather be afield.

Peter saw the grim finality of it. Samarc wasn't changed. He meant to end it. It was not only Spenski, but the havoc under the cloths....

A young assistant surgeon at a near cot was rather too hastily laying bare the lint from a severe shoulder wound.

Exchange with Samarc had of course stopped. Peter, thinking deeply, watched with but half attention until the assistant surgeon briskly rebound the wound, and began tugging at the soldier to get on his feet. The wounded one whimpered his weakness.

"Get up!"

The order was repeated. "Into your clothes, man. Scores are already in the column with wounds worse than yours."

The man groaned, stirred, but fell back. Peter had seen the wound—not a desperate one, but enough to lay a man up for a fortnight at home, and this could not have been more than three days old. There wasn't much chance of malingering.

"Come, come!" the young officer urged angrily.

The soldier tried to raise himself, but did not make good work of it.

"I'll get you up, damn you—"

A quick scream from the man on the cot. Peter did not know what the doctor did, but he smelled acid. All was cloudy before his eyes. He was a bit surprised a second after to feel the Russian's neck in his two hands:

"None but a beast would take from the stable a horse crippled like that," he was saying.

The assistant was but a boy. Peter caught this before lasting damage was done. He left the place half crying, threatening to kill Mowbray later. His superior appeared. Peter smiled at him. Samarc was up, drawing on his clothes.

"A bit of bad judgment," Peter said, not explaining whether it was his or the young doctor's.

The surgeon did not ask, but turned to the great muffled face.

"This man was from one of the rapid-fire commands, I believe?"

Peter was prevented from further glibness by a decisive nod from Samarc.

"The Fatherland will need you to-day," the surgeon said with a peculiar significance.

To Peter's trained ear the sounds from Samarc were dangerously like, "Fatherland-hell."

"A shrapnel splinter struck him in the mouth," he explained.

"He says he is ready to take the field."

Samarc spoke again.

"His blouse is gone," said Peter hastily. "I can manage for him."

"Has he a fever?"

"I'm afraid so—a slight fever."

The surgeon turned to the other cot. "Let this fellow sleep another day," he said.

The soldier lying there gave Peter a look almost uncanny in its gratitude.

"Sit down, Samarc. I'll get you a blouse," the latter said and left the ward.

Chapter 4

Big Belt awoke early in his own quarters, and beat around under the blankets for his friend. Peter was not there. Boylan remembered and sat up. This was the day of the great battle, but there was to be breakfast first. He recalled what was in the saddle-bags. This proved unsatisfactory. Even that hinged on Peter, as every thought so far. ... Boylan now reflected that he might have stayed longer in the ward last night. There was just as much to hold him to the cot of Samarc as had called Peter. Altogether, the day was not beginning in a way to suit,

He sat in the center of a tired tangle of woolen blankets and buckled on his leggings. His face pricked his chest as he bent forward. There was a stabbing run of ideas that had to do with marble baths, tepid plunges and fragrant steam. This collection he made haste to banish with matters of the day, and the absence of Peter,—but the pictures were various and persistent—exceptionally enticing baths from all his history recurring. He stretched out his gray woolen shirt and brushed it hard with handfuls of dried grass; he washed uncomfortably. It was like an ablution before one is undressed— that pervasive beard affair—and a general chill and dampness about clothes and boots that had not yet worked warm. The day was alternate gray and red. Noise gained in the street. Big Belt stepped forth.

Just at this moment he saw Peter Mowbray disappear into that grim street entrance from which the unspeakable human outcry had issued yesterday. He followed, twisting into doorways to let provision wagons pass, quickening his steps to cross between detachments of infantry. A certain dead cavalry horse was powerful in the air. Boylan knew exactly where it lay, for it had called attention these three days, an

Austrian property, saddle and all, a ghastly outpouring upon the turf.

Boylan found himself stepping forward with a gladness that was answered with sharp objection by his own nature, and which he would not have let Peter Mowbray know for all Judenbach. He was disgusted with the weakness that made a man friend such a profound institution in his breast.

The hall-way was dark. Boylan heard low voices; something from them prevailed to hush his entrance. In fact, at the turning he stood quite still for possibly three seconds. Beyond in the shadows Peter stood with a woman. Afterward Boylan recalled that there had been one poignant cry of pain from above, as if born of the monotone of moaning in that house.

They did not see him.... A little man appeared from the shadows, joined the two, and handed Peter a Russian blouse such as is worn by hospital stewards of the service. Peter thanked him; the other departed; the two were once more alone.... The huge scarred head of the old war-wolf withdrew jerkily; with stealth, he stepped back into the street. He did not stop until he reached his own quarters. There he found that he had not folded his blankets. In the midst of this work his hands stopped.... He was as accustomed as any man can be to unremoved horse by this time. It came steadily to his nostrils, mingled with the leathery smell of his own field-outfit. Presently he looked at his watch, and snapped the case shut with a crack. The strength of his fingers would have broken a filbert.

"Some men can find 'em anywhere," he muttered. "And such a one! She was a flame.... As for Mr. B. B.—it's dead horse all his days."

Chapter 5

Ashamed of himself, Big Belt waited to see if Peter would turn in to their quarters, as he approached carrying the hospital steward's blouse across his arm. Boylan would not call. It was like a woman's way—to learn if a man had forgotten her; still he would not call.... Clean-shaven, very straight and full of life, Peter approached, smiling at packers and soldiers, a smile for all the world. "Why not?" Boylan thought. Peter did turn in, and came toward him, hand out.

"Tomato ketchup with duck's eggs. Draw up a chair," said Boylan. He appeared just now to see the steward's blouse.

"Samarc takes the field to-day. It's for him," Peter explained.... "He's going out to kill himself. Only one reservation—that he kill no one else."

Boylan seemed staring at Peter's knees.

"You're letting the ketchup burn," Peter said mildly.

"I suppose that's what he really means to do," Big Belt observed, after a moment. "And what are we to do about it?"

"I thought I would stand by a little—not so as to be a nuisance, you know—"

"Naturally not. Of course."

They ate in silence—a thousand things to say.

"I won't be very far from the staff," said Peter, hurrying back to the hospital. "Poor old Samarc has two wounds, you know—"

* * *

It wasn't a day to explain things—not a day to talk. Men afield can never tell what they are doing; some devilish irony is in the air. They laugh; they listen; they hope—only a jest comes. The most thrilling and stupendous situations bring forth but a curse or a roar. Human throats are inarticulate, afield; the reality that voices heroic utterance and makes it memorable is not at work in man-fabric; splendid faces and brave actions—but the words are the revealers of emptiness. For the animal is awake and upstanding; the spirit that quickens reality is apart.

The battlefield opened to Mowbray's eyes that day with abnormal clearness, as if he had brought rest and reflection to a problem that long had harried him, He felt singularly light and full of ease—as one does sometimes in the first hours of the day after a sleepless night. The day was wild with west wind, a touch of south still clinging. The east arrayed itself again and again in all the delicate blends of pink and gray, watery yellow, rose, and azure; a different arrangement at each glance, as if separate groups of maidens followed each around a Roman bath.

Samarc was given a seat in an ammunition wagon, with orders to join his battery. Peter found his horse, already saddled by Boylan, and overtook the wagon train as it left the town. In a halt for the way to clear, Kohlvihr and his staff passed, Dabnitz and Boylan riding together. The General sat soft and lumpy in the saddle, his eyes small and feverish, his face hotly red. The staff passed on, all except Boylan believing that the correspondent had fallen in behind. Riding

Will Levington Comfort

with the wagons, Peter frequently turned to the terrifying bandage above the steward's blouse. When the light was right, he caught a glint of the eyes beneath.

The way became steep for the wagons as they neared the emplacements. Peter swung off and led his pony. Infantry was already engaged down in the hollows; the reek of powder began to cut the air at intervals, but the strong wind as often cleansed it away, and the scent of woods came up startlingly, with the warmth of the sun upon the ground—the sweet healing breath of drying cedar boughs.

He was sorry now he had roughed it with the young doctor; that sort of thing was very far from him. He had no memory of another episode like it. On occasion, dropping into the queerest abstractions, he fancied *her* near.... It had been like a soldier leaving his lady for the battle—the precious few minutes less than an hour ago. She had promised to be with him. There had been no talk nor thought of the terrifying day she faced in the hospital; everything had to do with his taking the field. She would follow him with her thoughts. Perhaps he would find his soul out there, she suggested, as he had never found it before. Peter wondered now just what she meant by that. It was not his way to fall back upon any such abstraction.

He reflected how her presence always changed him, gave him strength of a different sort, and directness of aim.... It was true that she seemed near—on the other side from Samarc—a part of the mountain fragrance that would not be overpowered in the gun-reek. He felt if he could turn quickly enough he would catch the gleam of her colors. This was her country. She was of the north and the cold lands; she belonged to the purity of the cedars.

He played with the thought that she was near; and from the

thought, because it was good, a glimpse of the future came to him—the peace to come, when men would dwell again with their loves, and the dream of superb affiliation would come true. All this madness of men would pass, as the rising powder-reek would pass from these Galician hills, and leave them their silence and their natural fragrance.

The wagons had gone on. Samarc's battery might have been rubbed out for all their ability to find it. All faces strange—gunners, range-finders, and the cartridge hands. Peter felt a horror in his breast for the immediate presence of the guns—as if he had reached the end of toleration in the one day with them. Samarc felt this hate, too, his ruling passion.... Any moment one of the rapid-firers might drum into action. Their sense was one—that something would be uncoupled in their minds. They turned, Peter laughing at his desire to run—as they found another group of machines emplaced in a rocky shelter a little higher than the spot where the shrapnel had struck three days before.

No one called to them as they turned back. A small belated wagon train rumbled by, but no one hailed them from the seats. They were free, alone. Peter inhaled the scent of the forest, sharp again from the acrid taint of the cool, hazy air. He loved the sweet mountain wind as never before—almost as if he were to leave it all. There was little need of exchange of words. Each understood mainly the thoughts of the other. Big guns thundered at each other from the remoter hills. Again they saw an infantry movement start forth below—the endless strings of infantry along the broad lower slopes. They stopped to watch them.

Creatures of the hollows, their business to rise and be swept back—marching forth now—Kohlvihr's command. Peter's eyes filled and his throat stopped at the spectacle of the gray lines. Surely something was the matter with him, he thought.

Was it pathological—loss of sleep, or fatigue? Or was it something that Spenski and Abel, the field and hospital; more than all was it something that Berthe Wyndham had given him? In any event, it seemed as if those infantry lines marching out now to the burning front were being torn from his own breast, every *moujik* precious. He wanted to be with them, not with the heinous guns. He wished he could spare them, stop the continual sacrifice. Miles of gray lines moving out now. ...His companion's tugging hand.

It dawned upon Peter before many sounds that Samarc wanted to go alone. He pointed the trail back around the hills toward Judenbach, where it would meet the road Kohlvihr had taken, suggesting that Peter join the staff. He, Samarc, would continue the search for his battery. As a rule Mowbray was the last to continue in the presence of a man who wanted him to go; and yet, he knew that Samarc hated the field pieces as much as he, and that he did not mean to live through the day. He hesitated. The final urging was pitiful— a sort of tumult from under the cloths.

"Nothing doing, Samarc," he said suddenly. "You and I for it—at least a while yet. I say—do the hard thing. The little man would have it so. We'll go down closer to the infantry stuff and forget ourselves."

...Yes, Samarc would do the hard thing. There was gratitude for which Peter had no receptivity—gratitude for the friendship, the night's watching. His hand was taken and carried to the other's breast, as only a Russian could do—and down they went together.

The infantry was their magnet as they made the down grade—miles of gray lines. The lower land was trampled and dusty; the breeze lost itself in the hollows. Just as an orchardist, discovering a certain parasite on his trees, thinks of a specific poison, so they knew that this great "forward" of the Russian foot-soldiers would start the Austrian machine and rapid-fire batteries.

They were moving now in front of a long line of new Russian works which had appeared deserted. Boylan would have known better; Samarc should have known. Peter had taken for granted that these had been emptied by the huge advances already in movement. They were in the path of Kohlvihr's reserves, it appeared, in the center of the line, when the signal "forward" was sounded. The works suddenly blackened with men. It was too much for the pony. Peter found a bridle with a broken throat latch in his hand, as he watched the little beast tear down the front, and heard the roar of laughter from the oncoming line.

The new front seemed endless in the rolling land. They were instantly enveloped. Out of the throng appeared one face that Peter had bowed to once or twice before—a captain, now working his way toward them. He glanced at the civilian insignia on Peter's sleeve, and said, with a smile:

"You've tricked us well this time, Mr. Mowbray. I hope you get back as cheerfully. You'll have to go forward now—at least, until we stretch out in skirmish. We're rather thick just here. Stay with my command—"

"We thought we were back of you," Peter said. "I assure you I didn't plan this, but it's very kind of you."

The Captain glanced at Samarc and turned to the American as they urged on.

"Hurt badly?"

"Just his face."

"Stay by—some of the soldiers might be rough—"

They were carried forward in the resistless interference of great numbers.

Chapter 6

Peter had pitied the infantry formerly from a hill, having stood with a battery as it sprayed the Austrian lines. He had watched the Austrian machines pouring steel upon the Russians also. There had been emotion; he had felt the shame of it powerfully on this very morning; but now he reflected, with a touch of levity, that his pity had not been adequate. At the present juncture he belonged to the sacrifice. The process was reversed; the globe of his experience shortly to be made complete. He would have the effects of light and darkness from the vantage of the preying and the preyed upon.

Peter had never been actually down among men before. He had watched men, studied them sincerely, passed them in the street, reflected upon their problems. At the same time, his personal impetus had always been away from men, his a different purpose, a different aim. He was *one* now, one in the massed destiny of the command, one to obey. Only by falling could he be free from this extraordinary authority of the army.

Moreover, he felt that the motive energizing this authority was not of the human but of the tiger.

He might have thought of all this before, as he had thought of death as one thing for the outsider and a different thing for the little lens-maker he liked so well. But this was experience, not conjecture. He was an atom of the charge. The army authority disrupted his moral sense. It bound and gagged him. No imagination could have constricted his vital and creative force as this adventure, in which he was caught up like a chip and carried forward in a rush of animal power. Fear had no part of his revulsion, but the break of his will. It

Will Levington Comfort

was not like a man drowning, in an insensible element; this that carried him *had* a consciousness and it was unclean.

He saw that the rankers leaned on each other; that there was not yet in the peasant faces about him a single separate individual relation to the impending peril. These men might have, seen others fall by the hundreds, but their faith was in the command, their law its law. Peter saw that they were in a sense like men parading through city streets, who endure the eyes of the crowds because they are part of a line. It was the eternal illusion of numbers again—the elbow brush, the heat, the breath, the muttering of men—this atmosphere that the military machine breathed. Standing alone, most of them would have fallen from fear.

He smelled the unwashed crowd. Under all the bronze that life in the open had given the command was the lardy look of earth-born men, close-to-the-ground men; these were the hordes that put on pounds and size, the rudiment of a mind, the momentary ignition of soul perhaps in moments such as now—and pass to the earth again. Yet the history of Europe was to be written upon a surface like this; this, the soil of the future. It was close to chaos, but as yet undefiled by man. This was the newest product of earth, the new terrific fecundity of the North that had alarmed lower Europe; these were the peasant millions as yet unfathered, strong as yet only as bulls are strong, gregarians, almost without memory; their terror, pain, passion, hope, genius not individual yet, but in the solution of the crowds.

Peter Mowbray's shock was the loss of the sense of self; his battle to retain this sense. He seemed to fuse in the heat, the vast solution draining his vitality. He could have given himself to the white fire of a group of men like Spenski, Abel, Fallows, Poltneck, perhaps—but to give himself to this.... They were stretching out now as skirmishers, the crush ended. Entire figures of men could be seen, instead of necks, beards, and shoulders. Samarc gripped his arm, the other hand pointing to a little red-haired boy who ran, crouched, sped on again, halted to look, in the true squirrel fashion of advance, which is the approved procedure of skirmishers. He talked to himself, appeared lost in absorption, reminded one continually of Spenski when his face was averted—and was just one of the miles of infantry.

Their faces looked cold now; a part of the gray tone so often observed. The officers fought to stretch them out. Every line of fear that the human mouth can express Peter saw. Now the drum of the Austrian pieces. It was not as they had heard it in the heights, but like an encore at first—as if some tremendous mass of men in a wooden gallery had started a buffeting of feet. The valley muffled the volleys; the actual steel was not heard until it neared like a rain torrent; indeed it found their immediate lines before they heard the murderous cutting of the air. The Austrian gunners were placed for enfilading, so that a fraction of point gave them impaling force and a wide swath in the ranks.

Peter saw the little red head cocked forward as if to listen to the nearing gusts of steel.

Now men were down and crying out. The fire was like that of a hostile regiment concentrating its volley upon a little knot of soldiers—the air was whipped, wild with throbbing missiles. Supernatural fear was the answer from the very souls of men. Their prayer (in Mowbray's conception) was not for life, but for cessation. Yet the machines held them with infernal leisure as one holds the stream from a garden hose to a spot of clay clinging to masonry.

In all postures the soldiers met the gale, with every answering sound. Then falling, rising, crawling, the remnant went back. It was not pain nor death nor wounds that mattered—but the hurtling concussions in the air, the plague of steel....

It stopped. Peter lay exhausted an instant. He felt no hurt. He was down because one could not stand in that sweep of projectiles. He recalled that he had seen the red head fall a moment before, and turned like a sick man, his eyes rolling, to learn if it were a dream or not. Yes, Redhead had fallen. Samarc was crawling toward him on his knees. Peter writhed forward, too, but disliking the movement lest it bring the guns upon them again. He forgot that. Redhead was muttering about *the storm*.

"Are you hard hit, boy?" Peter called.

There were others about—a whole line of fallen, but they saw just this one—his cheek to the dirt, his mouth moving queerly. He was young like the undersurgeon, seventeen or eighteen, and much bewildered, the gray, clayey hue upon him, but not at all uncouth. Samarc felt his spine, turned him. The wound was in his body. Just now Redhead saw the effigy that was Samarc. He had been watching Peter before.

His mouth opened, eyes seemed to settle back into a red gleam of horror, his face swung around into the dirt. Peter would have given his arm to spare Samarc that. No sound from under the cloth—only a breath. Samarc shouldered him, raised himself with the burden.

There are pressures of will. One turns on a certain force to meet an obstacle, and it is exhausted. There are other sources of power, but one brushes death to summon them. Far ahead they saw the remnant making cover. Now Peter noted that there was human need at every step. They lay in all positions, squirmed their faces up to him and implored. The few were still; the many writhed. He looked for a small one. He had never lifted a man and was surprised when one came up and rolled as if by magic across his back. It was so easy that he wanted to take others.

"I will come back," he called to the faces.

He meant to come back as he said it. He wanted to bring them all in. He had no hate for the Austrian gunners, because he had seen Samarc and Spenski at the same work, and he knew that the heart of man changes in a day. He would have helped the little undersurgeon had he been there. A *moujik* arose from his knees in front of them, as they staggered on. He was stunned, bewildered, blinded, but he could hear.

"Come on—we're going back," Peter said.

The other held out his hand gropingly. Peter placed the flap of his coat in it, and the moujik stumblingly followed.... Another soldier on his knees barred the way.

"We're going back," Peter said. "Come on. You can crawl—"

The soldier set out eagerly to obey, as if it had been a great boon to follow with his own strength. It was the mightiest episode of the day to Peter Mowbray. "My God, how they obey *men*!" he said, with awe. "They *could* be led right— peasants who obey like that!"

There was singing all about him—not of bullets, though this little movement on the field drew a thin, uncertain long-range fire from some intrenchment (apparently it was not enough to start a machine)—a low singing as of wells of gladness reaching the surface. Peter was torn with the agony of the field, yet thrilling with happiness—as if there was liberation somewhere within. He turned to the crawling one who inspired him:

"We're all hurt, but we're going back to bed. Come on—you're doing famously—"

The back bobbed to greater effort. The blind one held him fast, and the Redhead left his trail of blood and murmured about *the storm*.... It was a long range for the rifles, and seemed as harmless as sandflies after the horror of hornets they had known.... They were alone. They saw the heaped rims of the Russian works ahead—five of them, alone, for, queerly enough, they were as one.

And now from ahead, from the concealed Russian lines, arose a roar such as Peter had never known. It struck him with a psychic force that filled his eyes with tears, though he did not understand. He thought that the end of the war must have come—so glad and so mighty was that shouting.

Now a fragment of the line ran forth to bring the little party in, not minding Peter's gestures in the least; for he waved them back, lest they start the machines again.... It appeared that his little group of maimed and blind came home marching into the very hearts of the command—even the Red one.... They had laid their burdens down; an incoherent Boylan took Peter, leading the way back to the staff. Kohlvihr and Dabnitz stood there, the old man repeating:

"Get the name of the hospital man."

Dabnitz plucked the sleeve of Samarc's coat.

"Hospital steward,—I have that," he said a second time, "but what's the name and the division?"

"He can't speak," said Peter. "I'll get his name later. He's been wounded in the mouth."

Curiously enough in this turmoil it appeared for the first time why Samarc had been allowed a free field practically—why he had not been impressed for service by one of the batteries. It was the steward's blouse that Abel had given him.... Peter lost wonder at this. Things were darkening about him. He smelled the cedars. Her colors seemed just out of view.... She had been near.

"Peter—are you hit?" It was Boylan's voice.

"No, just bushed."

Now he heard Kohlvihr say: "Anything for you we can, Mr. Mowbray. As a civilian, you are of course exempt from specific honors, but as soon as I learn your companion's name I shall suggest that he be honored by the Little Father."

"Why, you've put the whole line back into fighting trim!" Boylan whispered.

Will Levington Comfort

Chapter 7

Something of the activity now apparent to the blurred faculties of Mowbray, as he sat in the clammy embrace of nausea and struggling for breath, appealed to him as structurally wrong; almost inconceivably abominable, in fact. He had no interest in his so-called achievement, regarded it with a laugh, repeated that it was pure accident; but such as it was, he objected to it being used to put the line back into "fighting trim."

He was in the large sod-covered pit occupied by field headquarters. He turned at the sound of breathing at his side. Samarc was sitting there. Peter's hand went to his knee. Aides, messengers, and orderlies hastened in and out. There were twenty men in the pit—Kohlvihr the center of all. Big Belt was ministering—a flask, a momentary massage, a steady run of comment, ruddy from the heart.... The activity came to him again.

Kohlvihr was actually planning another infantry advance.

Peter started to speak, but halted for further reflection, a bit skeptical as to his own sanity. This was the third day of the battle; this the day planned to drive a hole through the difficult Austrian hills; the whole Russian army was dependent upon taking this Austrian position; the weather was becoming colder, Berlin still afar off; the Russian left and center pinned to the results of action here.

So far mental processes seemed adequate, but this changed in no way his attitude toward the atrocious activity in the brain of Kohlvihr of the bomb-proof pit.

Kohlvihr might sally forth for his wounded; hundreds were

dying out there in the windy hollow. He, Peter Mowbray, had seen their faces—their bodies to the end of sight. But Kohlvihr had no thought of that; rather to meet the range of death machines again with another horde of his skirmishers—and again—and again, until the end of the day—until enough passed through to gain the opposite slopes in fighting force, or until the Austrian ammunition was exhausted....

And Kohlvihr had never been out there. His cave was well back in the shelter of the works—sheltered from ahead and from the sky, with Judenbach behind.... Old Doltmir, the second in command, was saying:

"It's a terrible price to pay, General—a terrible price. You will note that they enfilade our lines as we reach the bottom land. You will note that their machines cover the valley perfectly and that they are practiced now—"

There was balm in that, but acid covered it an instant later from Kohlvihr, who swallowed a drink and turned with a snarl.

"We have the price to pay—"

Peter was thinking now of the front line that had cheered his coming in; the men so ready to forget themselves for a little spectacle, and the thrill that had come to his own breast from their shouting. *He loved them and knew why.* And those men, their lives and deaths—were in the hands of this red-eyed human rat who fouled the air.... No, Peter thought, it wasn't the brandy that smelled. It's Kohlvihr and the brandy.

"Good God, Boylan," he muttered in English, "can't you get him by the throat?"

Will Levington Comfort

Boylan's eyes were wild. He laughed softly, however, saying in Russian: "Very good, Peter—you'd joke at your death—"

And Big Belt's eyes roved to Dabnitz, who apparently had not heard Peter's remark.

...And now the tugging from Samarc that meant words! It seemed as if a ghastly stillness prepared for that final rumble; certainly stillness followed it. All eyes turned, even Kohlvihr's, to the effigy. But Peter alone understood.

"...Don't let them take off the bandages."

Samarc left his seat in the dark corner and walked evenly toward the center where Kohlvihr stood, his aides about him—poor old Doltmir standing apart and distressed. The moment had come for the order to be given. Kohlvihr turned to a dispatch rider at the door—a door made of cedar trunks.

For the moment Peter was blocked between two desires, or paralyzed. The huge face of Boylan close by mutely implored him to be silent.

"Samarc," he called.

Samarc did not turn. Now Peter saw the red face of Kohlvihr in its gray fringe suddenly lifted and enlarged. The effigy was close to it, but not higher, and hands were tightening beneath it—Samarc's strong unhurt hands. There had been one snarling scream. It was followed by a shot from Dabnitz. The red face went down with the other to the clay floor.

Chapter 8

The roar of the battle followed as Peter staggered back alone to Judenbach. He must have traversed a mile before there was a rational activity of his faculties. The first mental picture was that of the officers running along the works as the order for "advance as skirmishers" was given. They were inspiring the men in the name of the Little Father.

"If only they hadn't said that," Peter muttered pathetically.

Then he recalled that Kohlvihr had been lifted practically unhurt from the clay floor; that his order was carried out. The infantry had obeyed. With all he knew, and all he had seen that day, the mystery of common men deepened. Out of it all strangely stood forth in his mind now the man who could not rise, but who crawled after him at a word.... These men obeyed—that was the whole story. If they were given true fathers!... Why, that *was* the answer!

Peter had come into this with all the fire of revelation. He had earned it. Blood and courage, and the stress of death, had given it to him. Yet it was worth it all. He would tell Berthe Wyndham....

He stopped short at the edge of the town. Never was there in his life a moment of profounder humility. Berthe Wyndham had told him all this before they left Warsaw—on the day that the message came from Lonegan. All he had learned to-day through such rigor and jeopardy she had told him; and she had understood it then with the same passion that he had it now.

Peter had only listened that day; he had lived it to-day. His heart suddenly flooded with warmth for Fallows. Fallows had been through all this—all the burning and zealotry of it, and had come forth into the coldness and austerity of service. It was very wonderful. Peter Mowbray's eyes smarted. They, and the service, had certainly crumpled the old fronts of calm and the sterile pools of intellect. He loved the peasants now, *and he knew why....* He saw what a stick he had been, but this didn't trouble him greatly. The new seeing was enough; he was changed. His emotions presently concerned the fresh realizations so dearly bought—in the past three days... three days.

Not until now did he think of Samarc.... The reality had stood like a black figure at the door of his brain throughout all the walk, but it did not enter until now. No, Samarc would not come back to Judenbach. It was finished as he had intended. He had ceased to kill. Even at the last he had but used his hands, and in as righteous wrath as ever tortured human fingers to terrible strength.... He, Mowbray, had not remained to assure himself that the last command of his friend was obeyed. This hurt him not a little.... He was in the main street... exertion, sorrow, exaltation; now he was whipped again. He felt he had not done well at the last. A teamster yelled to him to get out of the way. Peter stepped back wearily to let a string of ambulances by.

Across was that grim door of the house of amputations. He was not quite ready to enter. He would get himself in hand better. He had not been gone long—it was only mid-forenoon. He would go to his quarters and clean up a little—perhaps rest a moment. His thoughts turned often to Samarc, always with a pang. He wished the Big Belt were here. This last reminded him of his saddle bags—razors and all gone with the pony. Boylan would have the laugh at him now.

He could not sit still in his quarters. Voices came to him

from the street, from the court—even from that grim place a little down the way. He arose and went across to the familiar hospital ward.... Another was in Samarc's place. A hand beckoned. It was from the cot of the soldier for whom he had struggled with the young doctor. He went to it. There was a message:

"They were talking of you as an enemy—"

That was all. Peter did not care for particulars. His volition was quickened. He had been sadly in need of that. Now he went direct to the hallway, where he had left her in the morning, and on upstairs. The rooms were crowded with wounded and medical officers, but no familiar face—neither Berthe Wyndham nor Moritz Abel.

Many eyes held him. He did not see the young doctor, but the surgeon who had come to the other ward was there—that bland, quiet face, regarding him curiously now. Peter asked nothing, and was free apparently to move anywhere about the building. None of his own was there. His loneliness was untellable. He could not have spoken to a stranger without a break of tone....

He wished for Boylan again.

Peter was in the street, moved along the walls as one very tired. He was searching, but the thoughts grew so terrible that he could not keep his eyes to outer activity. His steps led him to the Court of Executions. Standing by the street gate, he dreaded to enter. He would not tolerate this, yet it was more than life or death. He had a mental picture of finding her there, her body shrinking into one of the stone corners—as a maimed bird that has fallen lies still under its wings.

His breath burst from him. He had been holding it as if under water. His eyes traveled electrically now.

There were dead in the court, but she was not there, nor Abel nor Fallows. He looked through the row of gratings and under the arches. There was a low stone lintel with a dim deserted hall beyond....

Just now a step behind him, heavy boots ringing on the stone flags. Peter turned. A Russian soldier halted, raised his rifle, commanded him to advance.

Peter waved his hand in a gesture of obedience, but turned to glance in the gloom under the lintel again. It was just *in the turning* that he had caught the gleam of her colors—not when he stared straight in. Peter assured himself of this before giving himself up.

IV

IN THE BOMB-PROOF PIT

Chapter 1

The dead man in the hospital steward's coat had been carried forth from the bomb-proof pit.

Big Belt perceived that the day was working out according to its evil beginnings.... After coming in from the infantry hollows as one risen from the dead (and transfigured in the garish light of field bravery) Peter Mowbray had left him again, now in the possession of strange devils.

Boylan was not ready to go back to Judenbach. It was almost noon. He was watching the heart of the Russian invasion of Galicia, and from its main lesion. This he knew quite as well as Dabnitz, or Doltmir, or the half-insane Kohlvihr himself. The Austrians still held. Indeed, it was not hard for them. The Russian west wing entire, and possibly part of its center, would be called upon to flank this stoutly adhering force, if Kohlvihr continued to fail. Such an action would greatly delay the general forward movement of the Russian arms.

"You will be without a command, General," Doltmir

suggested, at the end of the second infantry throwback, following that in which Peter had participated. "We are not disturbing them greatly in our advances. We are chiefly effective in destroying their ammunition—"

"Then we must continue that," said Kohlvihr.

"But the troops will not continue to charge. Our reserves are in. The fresher men see the fate of the former advances. The hollows are in plain sight from the forward rifle pits."

"The officers must drive them forward—"

"Most of the lesser commanders are lying in the valley. The troops are killing them as well as the enemy—"

"Do you mean there is mutiny, sir?"

"Not of a reckonable type. These men work in the midst of action. Moreover, our troops are hard pressed. Our division has borne the brunt for three days in almost unparalleled action."

"Would you advise me to leave them funking in the trenches?" Kohlvihr demanded.

"General, I would advise a report to the Commander of our failure in four advances—that we can not get sufficient men across the valley to charge the Austrian positions. Meanwhile I would order the wounded to be brought in. After that, I would suggest food for the men in the trenches."

"I do not care to report four failures without a fifth trial."

Doltmir turned back.

Big Belt was thinking fast. In all his experience, he had never seen the Inside stripped naked like this. Of course, he had observed the strategy of small bodies of troops determined by a swift consultation of officers; but this was an army in itself, or had been, and on the part of Kohlvihr it was very clear that personal matters were powerfully to the fore. Kohlvihr was enraged; Kohlvihr was ambitious. Big Belt was aware that, given a free hand and a free cable, he could make Kohlvihr a loathsome monster in the eyes of the world, this merely by a display of the facts.

Boylan's view was cleared a little as he thought of such a narrative. His sense of the reception of the story showed him the commanding nature of it. The thing might be done later. Peter's trouble was that he could not forget it for the present. Thoughts of work put a new energy into Boylan's thinking. These things now passing in the bomb-proof pit formed the climax of a narrative that had been running from the Warsaw office to the present hour.... For a moment in the story's grasp, Boylan did not hear the voice of the invaluable Dabnitz:

"...He is under suspicion, sir," that young officer was saying to his chief. "In fact, the whole hospital corps is rotten with revolutionists, but the fact remains he can sing like an angel. I think if Poltneck were brought here to the lines and made to sing the folk songs—"

"Get him," said Kohlvihr. "Is he under arrest?"

"No; as yet merely under espionage. He was valuable in rather a unique way in the hospitals yesterday."

"Bring him at once."

Kohlvihr sent an order for his troops to rest and have a bite in the trenches.

The sorry Doltmir stepped forward again:

"Would it not be well to bring in our wounded from the field, sir?"

"We will *have* the field presently," said Kohlvihr. "The sun is not hot. The lines already have seen too much of their blood."

Big Belt remembered that. Moments were intense again when Poltneck was brought in—a tall, angular, sandy-faced chap, with a wide mouth and glistening teeth, a smile that quickened the pulse, somehow. Boylan thought of the passions of women for such men. His shoulders were lean and square. Yellow hair, long on top and cropped tight below the brim of his hat, dropped a lock across his forehead, as he uncovered in the bomb-proof pit. He had been shaven-recently. Boylan reflected that he belonged to the hospital corps. There was a thrill about him not to be missed.

"Poltneck—he calls himself," Dabnitz whispered. "Poltneck perhaps, but I've seen him with the Imperial orchestra or I'm losing memory. I didn't have a good look at him before—"

Dabnitz was called by the General, who was seated with Doltmir over a small collation with wine and bread. The lieutenant was requested to arrange the inspiration for the men in the trenches.

Boylan noted how much taller the singer was than even the tall Russian officer—as the two stood together.

"The men are very tired, Poltneck," Dabnitz began. "Much has been required of them, and much is still required. We want you to help us."

"Yes?"

Poltneck had been looking about, interested as a kitten in a strange house. He regarded Kohlvihr and the rest, the trace of a smile around his mouth. The smile was still there as he turned quickly to Dabnitz with the single questioning word, not contemptuous in itself, but Boylan imagined it morally so. The voice furnished a second and very real thrill.

"We thought you would sing for your fellow soldiers. You are from the peasantry, I am told?"

"Yes, from the people."

"We thought you would understand," Dabnitz added. "There is an operatic tenor in the command—one Chautonville. We might have sent for him, but our thought was to reach the soldiers directly. It is a great honor."

"Is it? How and where do you want me to sing?"

"An advance is to be ordered immediately. We will send an escort with you along the trenches—just before the order is given. I heard you singing yesterday. I am sure the men will answer with zeal."

Poltneck seemed to wilt. Boylan was caught with the others thinking it was the mention of the trenches that frightened this hospital soldier. Yet the smile had not changed when Boylan's eye roved to that. It was not more contemptuous, nor less; but something about it was unsteadying. Dabnitz already had used many more words than he expected.

"I am not used to crowds," Poltneck objected weakly. "I am

just a simple man. Already I am without voice. I beg of you to send for Chautonville of the opera."

Dabnitz was puzzled.

"That is out of the question. Chautonville is back in the city. Within twenty minutes the order for advance will be given. Come, Poltneck; you will do very well when you see your soldiers—"

Boylan reflected swiftly at this point that the smile might be neither deep nor portentous—a single accomplishment, some stray refinement perhaps that had leaked back somehow to the people.

"No, no. I am afraid. I belong back among the wounded. I am very good there. This is not my place—"

"Will you require men to assist you to the trenches? Already I have talked too long."

"Yesterday I was an anesthetic," Poltneck wailed. "To-day I am to be a stimulant."

Kohlvihr now came forward. "It is time," he said.

"General," said Dabnitz, "we have to deal with an unusual peasant, I am afraid."

"It would not do for me to encroach upon the work of professionals," the singer explained in dilemma.

"You see he is humorous," Dabnitz observed.

"We sent for you to sing to the soldiers. Will you do that?" the General asked, from puffing cheeks.

Poltneck looked down at him with sudden steadiness. "On the way home," he said.

"You refuse—then?"

"I would prefer that you wound them first."

"At least, he has declared himself," said Dabnitz.

Chapter 2

They did not murder him then and there. Boylan was glad of that. His sack was already full of blood.... It was all too big. Something would happen to spoil the telling. No man ever got out with such a story.... He was a little ashamed to find himself thinking of his newspaper story so soon after the singer was led forth—the man who would sing for the wounded, but who would not sing men to their death. Come to think—there was a prostitution about it. Certainly Poltneck had a point of view. And he was a hair-raiser of quality... everything about him.

Boylan thought of writing the Poltneck incident, and became hopeless again. The Russians would be idiots to let him out alive. He did not expect it. The only chance was that they couldn't see themselves. Perhaps Kohlvihr thought he was a hero to-day. Doubtless he did.... One thing was sure, he, Boylan, must sit tight with his enthusiasm for the Russian force; must play it harder than ever—must play it for Peter Mowbray, too.

"You fellows certainly have your troubles—front and back," he said to Dabnitz. "But I say, Lieutenant, you couldn't ask troops to go forward better—you couldn't ask more of the Japanese in the business of charges—"

"I wasn't out in that service," Dabnitz observed.

"Grand little bunch of celibates afield, those Japanese— religious about these matters of using up hostile ammunition. Fact is, I never saw white troops go out to a finish four times in one day—as yours did to-day—out over their own dead, too—"

He was becoming genial; his heart quaking for Peter, as he thought suddenly of the words aimed at Kohlvihr's throat, and of Peter's association at the last with the man in the steward's blouse. ...Dabnitz was unvaryingly courteous.

The advance was on again. Boylan went forth to see the repulse. The main lines on either side had loosened to fill the gaps of Kohlvihr's division, the much-torn outfits braced by the fresher infantrymen. On they went, a last time, over the strewn land.

Boylan saw it all again; heard the drum of the batteries when the troops reached the hollow of the valley; saw them change like figures on a blurred screen; perceived the antics and the general settling—and turned away....

It was like the swoop of a carrion bird an instant afterward— and the deafening strike. The Austrians had varied a little. A shrapnel battery had been emplaced among the rapid-fire pieces during the recent interval. A hundred yards down the works to the east landed the first finger of a hand that groped for headquarters. Boylan watched for the second shell—one eye, and as little besides as possible, above the rim of the trench now deserted. It was the same tension and tallying of seconds that Peter had known on the afternoon that the moon rose before the setting sun. Big Belt ducked at the second scream. The explosion was nearer and a little back. He returned to field headquarters just as a third shrapnel shivered the land still nearer the bomb-proof pit.

Kohlvihr's face was gray as the fringe of his hair. He looked little and aged.

"My compliments to the commander," he was dictating, "...report that after five advances we find enemy's front impregnable to infantry. Headquarters now under shrapnel fire. We are forced to withdraw toward Judenbach—"

The dispatch rider was standing by. The dirt sprinkled down on their heads through the wooden buttresses as another shrapnel broke outside.

"But the wounded, General. The field is alive with wounded—" came from Doltmir.

"I can't send troops out there again—" The voice was thick and hoarse with repression. "We'll get them at nightfall.... Gentlemen, we may now withdraw."

Boylan was one of the last to leave. He saw the aged legs disappear up the earth-rise as the rear door opened. The legs jerked and twitched spasmodically, as if taking an invisible spanking.

Boylan was actually afraid of his thoughts, lest they be read in his face—the shocking personal business on Kohlvihr's part. "A little shrapnel or two sends him quaking home, and *they* went out five times for him into the very steam of hell."

His brain kept repeating this in spite of him, so that he did not try to overtake the staff.

And *they*—the poor last fragment of them—were piling back toward Judenbach, leaving their wounded behind.

Chapter 3

Goylan was back in Judenbach. It was four in the afternoon. He had searched everywhere for Peter Mowbray. The whole war zone was getting blacker and blacker to his sight. He had even gone to the Grim House to look for the white-fire creature who had taken his companion to her breast, figuratively speaking; but neither she, nor the weak-shouldered little chap who had brought the hospital steward's blouse, was there. There remained Dabnitz, who more than any other was aware generally of what passed. Big Belt returned to headquarters and waited. Darkness was thickening before the Lieutenant came in.

"Where's Mowbray?"

Dabnitz came close and looked at the other sorrowfully.

"How long have you known Mr. Mowbray?"

Boylan tried to think. His faculties were at large. According to facts he had known Peter (and not at all intimately) during a mere ten weeks before the column left Warsaw. Facts, however, hadn't anything to do with the reality. Peter Mowbray was his own property. He said as much, his voice going back on him.

"Mr. Boylan, I have seldom been more hard hit. He was my friend, too. A more charming and accomplished young American would be hard to find, but we who are out for service, a life and death matter for our country, must not let these things enter. Mr. Mowbray is affiliated in various ways with our enemies—not the Austrians, but enemies more subtle and insidious."

Will Levington Comfort

"For God's sake—Dabnitz!"

"I thought it would hurt you."

"You might just as well say it of me."

"Not at all. Your record stands. It was well known to us when you were accepted to accompany our column. You will recall that it was your estimate of Mr. Mowbray's superior that decided us to accept the younger man—"

"I have been with Mowbray night and day. He is a newspaper man, brain and soul—one of the coolest and most effective I have ever met. He has been for years in Paris and Berlin, before Warsaw."

"I am sorry. You did not know that he caught a young surgeon by the throat this morning, when the former was very properly stimulating a malingerer?"

"I did not. But a personal matter ought not to weigh against a man's life—"

"You did not know that he was seen in somewhat extended conversation yesterday and last evening with one of the most dangerous of our recent discoveries among the revolutionists?"

"I did not."

"Or that a woman came to him last night, in the heart of the night—and talked long—and was called for by the same revolutionist; that Mr. Mowbray went to her a little after daybreak this morning—"

"Ah, Dabnitz—a little romance! All night he was serving in

the hospital. I went out to find him this morning, and saw him turn into the amputation house. Following, I saw him standing there.... He had probably never seen her until last night. You know how some young fellows are. They—you turn around—and they are in an affair—"

"But the two were overheard to speak of days in Warsaw together. It is not such a little affair."

"I know nothing of it, but is such a thing fatal?"

"She is under arrest with the other revolutionist that I mentioned—a case against her that is hardly breakable—"

Boylan sat down,

"Of course you are aware—of the remark he made this morning in the field headquarters? I saw how gallantly you tried to cover it. It was that remark, by the way, which nearly cost the life of our General. The hospital steward, took up the action as you know—"

"Dabnitz, I was shocked as you. Peter was beside himself. He had come in from the field—the actuality of it. He forgot where he was. The unparalleled energy of the General to win the day, you know—and Peter had just come in from the hollows where the men lay—"

"My dear Boylan, I'm sorry—"

For the first time, Big Belt felt the iron personality of the other. There was something commercial in the manner of the last, a kind of ushering out one who would not do. There are men who remain as aloof as the peaks of Phyrges, though their words and intonations come down running softly out of a smile. Boylan looked away, and then, with an inner groan, turned back.

"I tell you it is a mistake. The boy is as sound as—"

He couldn't finish. There were exceptions to everything he thought of. "I want to see him," he added.

"I'll try to manage that for you, a little later."

* * *

It was darkening. In the front room of the house, Kohlvihr sat bung-eyed by a telegraph instrument. The further strategy from Judenbach was still in the dark to Boylan. He wished the heavens would fall. As never before, he had the sense that he had pinned his life and faith to matters of no account; not that Peter Mowbray belonged to these matters, but that he, too, was meshed in them.... A shot from somewhere below in the town. Boylan shivered. There was shooting from time to time for various butchering reasons, but this particular shot was all Big Belt needed to finish the picture.

"Why, they'll shoot the lad," he muttered.

The sentence remained in his brain in lit letters.

The States of Americ a couldn't help him; even Mother Nature had turned her face from this war.... "My dear Boylan, I'm sorry—" something crippling in that.

Dabnitz returned, bringing a pair of saddle bags.

"They're Mr. Mowbray's," he said. "His horse got loose and tangled himself in a battery. One of the men brought in the bags."

"Thanks, Lieutenant," said Boylan.

Dabnitz started to the door when Boylan called, "Oh, I say, did you look through 'em?"

The Russian smiled deprecatingly.

"Of course, I needn't have asked that, but I wanted you to. I'll gamble you didn't find anything—"

"A little book of poems by a man we're familiar with. A woman's name on the front page—a woman we're familiar with. Nothing startling, Mr. Boylan."

Dabnitz was gone, the bags lying on the floor. Big Belt opened the nearest flap. On top was a case containing a tooth brush and a pair of razors.

"Peter will want these," he muttered.

V

THE SKYLIGHT PRISON

Chapter 1

Peter walked ahead unbound. He could not keep his mind on the journey with the sentry. His thoughts winged from Lonegan at Warsaw, to *The States'* office and home, as if carrying the message of his own end.... Boylan might finally break out with the details.... The personal part ended suddenly, like an essential formality, leaving him a sorrow for Boylan and his mother especially. His full faculties now opened to Berthe Wyndham.

He was ordered to turn twice to the left. They had left the little stone court, entering the main street, and back again into the first side street for a short distance to a narrow stairway, between low mercantile houses now used for hospitals. Up the creaking way; the sentry within answered the sentry without and opened the door. A long narrow room with a single square of light from the roof, and Moritz Abel came forward.

"I'm sorry," the poet said. "I had hoped—"

"Yes, we had hoped," Peter replied with a smile.

Duke Fallows appeared from the shadows and hastily pressed his hand. Abel had turned toward the square of light, as if there were still another.

She came forward like a wraith—into the light—and still toward him, her lips parted, her eyes intent upon him. The sentry who had brought him turned, clattered down the stairs. The door was shut by the other sentry. Her lips moved, but there was nothing that he heard. With one hand still in his, she turned and led him back under the daylight to the shadows.... He heard Moritz Abel's voice repeating that he had been a poor protector. Fallows spoke....

There was much to it, hardly like a human episode—the silence so far as words between them, the tragedy in each soul that the other must go; the tearing readjustments to the end of all work in the world, and the swift reversion of the mind to its innumerable broken ends of activity; and above all, the deep joy of their being together in this last intense weariness.... She wore her white veiled cap and apron; having followed the summons from her work. There was a chair in the shadows, and she pressed him down in her old way, and took her own place before him (as in her own house) half-sitting, half-kneeling.

"Peter, I could not believe—until I touched you. I was praying just here, that you would not come—"

"I am very grateful to be here," he said.

"I was so lonely. I was afraid of death. Fallows talked to me and Moritz Abel—but it did not do. I was thinking of you at the battle, as if you were a thousand miles away—as if I were waiting, as a mother for you, waiting for tidings with a babe in her arms—"

She paused and he said, "Tell me," knowing that she must speak on.

"...It was just like that. I prayed that you would live—that you would not be brought here—that the time would pass swiftly. We have been here hours. They came for us soon after you went. We were all together in that place—all at our work. They led us here through the streets. It seemed very far. Something caught in the throat when the soldiers looked at me. I know what my father felt when he kept saying, 'It's all right. Yes, this is all right.' I know just how the surprise and the amazement affected him from time to time, and made him say that.... Then we were here. I wanted this darker chair. They came—I mean our good friends—Fallows came and talked to me, and Moritz Abel, but it wasn't what I seemed to need. Ah, Peter, I'm talking in circles—"

Something warned him that she was going to break, but he could not speak quickly enough. The human frightened little girl that he had never seen before in Berthe Wyndham, was so utterly revealing to his heart that he was held in enchantment. She seemed so frail and tender, as she said plaintively:

"We must be very dear to each other—"

There were tears in her eyes now, and her breast rose and fell with emotion, as poignant to Mowbray as if it were his own.

"I did pray for them not to bring you here," she added. "If I had not left Warsaw, you would not be here now—"

"Listen—oh, Berthe, don't say that. Please, listen—"

The current was turned on in his brain, thoughts revolving

faster and faster:

"It would all have been a mere military movement if you had not come. I would not have understood Spenski, nor the real Samarc, nor Kohlvihr as he is, nor the charges of infantry. The coming of Moritz Abel, words I have heard, the street, the singing, the field, the future—why, it's all different because you came. I am not dismayed by this. I have had a great life here. If this is our last day—the matter is lifted out of our hands. And dear Berthe, what do you think it means to me—this last hour together?"

"What does it mean, Peter?'

"I look into your face, and know that I've found something the world tried to make me believe wasn't here. Everything I did as a boy and man tried to show me that there isn't anything uncommon in a man finding a woman. My mother knew differently, but every time she wanted to tell me something happened. Another voice broke in, or perhaps she saw I wasn't attentive or ready. But I know now—and it didn't come to me until here in Judenbach—"

"She must have known," Berthe whispered.

Fallows drew near. He seemed calm but very weary. "May I bring up my chair for a little while?" he asked as an old nurse might.

"Please do," they said.

"Thank you," Fallows answered, and returned with his wooden chair. "If you change the subject I shall have to go."

"I was just saying that I had found something in the world that my mother knew all the time," Peter explained.

"Oh, I say, this is important. Moritz must come in," Fallows told them.

They nodded laughingly.

"Moritz," he called. "Here's a little boy and girl telling stories—very important stories. You must hear.... We're all one, Peter Mowbray."

They drew closer together. Berthe was watching Peter intensely, knowing that it was his test, very far from his way. Then she remembered the death-room, and that all things are changed by that. She sat very still, trying to give him strength to go on. "I've always used my head," he said, "always explained why, and made diagrams. The one time I didn't use my head—well, the best thing happened in my experience."

Peter was in for it, and weathered gracefully.

"You'll forgive me," he said, when they asked to know. "I was thinking of meeting Berthe Wyndham. I saw her one day passing through the Square in Warsaw near the river corner. Well, it all came about, because I went there again the next day at the same time—"

He was a little breathless, but the glad and eager sincerity of his listeners helped him, and he wanted more than all to lift Berthe if he could.

"I could not help thinking of that when I recalled another little matter yesterday—in Judenbach. Once when we were little, my brother Paul and I quarreled. My mother and I were alone afterward. I told her of the tragedy. Everything seemed lost since I had lost Paul. She said, 'Some time you will find your real playmate, if you are good and search very hard.' I suppose she has forgotten. I forgot for years. But it came to me here.... You see I never suffered before, never was tested, everything came smoothly, everything covered up—"

"You are good to let us listen," Fallows said quietly. He was staring at the ceiling.

"Here in Judenbach the relations of all other days began to match up. It was as if the whole war was to show *me*, each department carried on clearly. I didn't know a man could stand so much. Day before yesterday morning, I wanted to quit. I had a kind of madness from it all—an ache that wouldn't break or bleed, and was driving the life out of me. I found the way out by going into the hospital. I had to forget myself or go under.... When it seemed all over to-day, and the sentry was marching me here (you see I had gone back to the house of amputations and couldn't find any of you, and then to the Court of Execution, and you were not there), it was all slipping away in a loneliness not to be described, when I found you here—"

Fallows straightened his head and blinked.

"'It was all slipping away in a loneliness not to be described,'" he repeated. "We know that. This is too fine."

Peter laughed. He was thinking of what Lonegan had said on the night he came back from Berthe's door, after she had asked him not to come in.... "Peter, you're lying. I don't believe you'd let anybody see your fires—not even how well you bank 'em."

They seemed to require further talk from him. He did not want the two men, sorry they had drawn up their chairs. His heart was very tender to them—Fallows and Abel, and the woman who had changed him. They were before him now as

Will Levington Comfort

messengers from the benignant empire of the future—strange strong souls gathered together now in waiting at the end of a road.... He told them of the bomb-proof pit, the naked animalism of Kohlvihr, the infantry advances and of Samarc. Presently his heart was light again, the pent forces of expression springing gladly into use.

"...The laughable thing about it," he finished, "—the thing that held me speechless as Samarc left my side there in the dark corner of the pit—was that just a few minutes before Kohlvihr had promised to see that the Little Father decorated him. He had almost reached the General when my throat worked, and I called, 'Samarc.' It was as if he didn't hear me. Nothing would have stopped him. It was his idea, yet I think he meant only to stop the order of another infantry advance. He had ceased to kill, you know...."

Peter ended it hastily. They were all interested to know why Samarc was to have been decorated. This opened the earlier part of the day, and his strange wandering with Samarc among the hills—the magic of the hospital steward's coat, the scent of the cedars, and Peter's persistent sense of Berthe's nearness.

"Actually, I had to stop and think," he explained. "Each time I fell into an abstraction, it struck me that she was there. It seems yesterday, too—"

"I was just here," Berthe said. "It was soon after we came. We were all quiet at first—in different corners—"

"Slipping away in that loneliness," Fallows suggested.

"As for me," said Moritz Abel, "I had to make peace with myself. We have been very busy the last few days. I have discovered that I am a bit of a coward at heart—and I missed having something to do—"

They smiled at him. "Perhaps I was out there," Berthe said. "Perhaps I was only sitting here—"

It was a queer matter that the three men, each of whom would have given his life to save the woman's, to all appearances accepted the fact of her as one of them in courage and control. It was Abel who mentioned the singer, Poltneck, whom Peter had not met. He had been left in the hospital when the others were taken; yet he had been one in all their interests and the most reckless and outspoken of all in his hatred of slaughter. They did not understand, but hoped he would be saved.

"He's a magician," Abel said. "He sang to them yesterday— as they bore the knife. He seemed to hold them in the everlasting arms. It was worth living to witness that, but I'm afraid Poltneck will come to us. He's got the fury. Hearing that we are gone, he will start something—if only to join us. Then there will be no one to escape with the story. It troubles me.... If Mr. Mowbray were only free. Doesn't it seem that our brothers should hear the story?"

His voice broke a little. His brow was wet.

Fallows came back from the ceiling, and said:

"Moritz, my boy, all is well with us. That which is true is immortal."

Will Levington Comfort

Chapter 2

Abel reflected.

"Yes," he said presently, "but we have not fulfilled our purpose.... You know, we set out in high courage to start the army back home again—and now, here we are."

"A man named Columbus set out to discover a short passage to India and found a New World. Really my son—these are not our affairs. We have done what we could.... Once I wanted the world to answer abruptly to my service—to speak up sharp. But I have made terms—hard terms we all must make. This is it—to do our part the best we can, and keep off the results. They are God's concern, Moritz."

"I dare say."

"When I was younger," Fallows went on, "I wanted to make a circle of light around the world. I thought they must see it, as I did. And often I left my friends discussing my failure. But once I came home and looked into the eyes of a little boy—a little peasant child named Jan. I saw that his love for me had awakened his soul.... Man, these matters are managed with a finer art than we dream of. The work is the thing." Peter swung into the larger current. They had all been cold. Fallows was burning for them. The ice and the agony were melting from each heart.

"We think all is going wrong. We sit and breathe our failures often when the celestial answer is in the air. If we were not so obtuse and fleshly, we could see the quickening of light about us. We have had our hours here. We have breathed the open. A very huge army is about us, and we are thrust aside. It would seem that we and our little story are lost in the great brute noise. Why, Moritz, these things that we have thought and dreamed will rise again in the midst of a world that has forgotten the tread of armies."

They heard a voice in the street—a running step upon the stair. Queerly it happened in that instant of waiting, that Peter heard the sound of dropping water beyond the partition—drip, drip, drip, upon a tinny surface. Berthe had risen, and followed Fallows and Abel to the door. A moment later Poltneck, the singer, was with them, and the sentry who brought him took his post with the other at the entrance. He freed himself from them, and strode alone to the front of the room, where he sat, face covered in his hands, weaving his head to and fro.

"You do not well to welcome me," he groaned at last. "I should have been in a cell alone—not here among friends. You see in me the most abject failure—a mere music-monger who forgot his greater work."

"Tell us—"

He did not answer at once. They led him back into the shadows where Peter and Berthe had been; gathered closely about, so their voices would not carry.

"We were hoping not to see you, said Abel, "yet sending our dearest thoughts. What you have done is good, and we will not be denied a song. Speak, Poltneck—"

"I was all right till you went. I was thinking of everything— but then I became blind. The work in the hospitals palled. I did not do what I could. They saw I was different, and watched closely. That made me mad. I am a fool to temper and pride. All I have is something that I did not earn— something thrust upon me that makes sounds. The rest is emptiness. In fact there must be emptiness where sounds come from—"

"We know better than that," said Fallows. "Tell us and we will judge."

Poltneck straightened up and met the eyes of Peter. "This is the correspondent?" he asked.

"He came up from the field this morning and in looking for us—fell under suspicion," Berthe explained.

The long hard arm stretched out to Peter, who still was somewhat at sea, as Boylan had been, and afraid that he detected a taint of the dramatic.

"I saw your companion in the bomb-proof pit," Poltneck declared. "In fact, I just came from there, but I will tell you.... I was perhaps two hours or more in the hospital, after you three were taken, when they sent for me. I thought it a summons, of course, such, as you—"

He glanced at the faces about him, and continued:

"But instead of leading me in the direction you had taken, the sentry bade me mount a horse at the door, and we rode rapidly down to the edge of the valley, to Kohlvihr's head-quarters—a pestilential place sunken in the ground and covered with sods. There they broke it to me what was wanted—"

His listeners began to understand.

"Yes, I was to sing to the lines," Poltneck added. "It appears they had been driven back several times, leaving their dead and wounded in such numbers on the field—officers and men—that there was some hesitation about the expediency of trying it again. Not, however, in the bomb-proof pit. Kohlvihr was of a single mind, determined to make his reputation as man-indomitable at the expense of his division. A patchy old rodent of a man—

"I was to be used to sing the men forward. Great God, they didn't see the difference from singing to wounded men, to men under the knife without sleep, to dying men and to homesick bivouacs—from this that they asked. It is my devil. I played with them. I made them think I was afraid. I made them think I was simple. One of them told me of the tenor Chautonville with the army. I played to that. It was very petty of me to get caught in this cleverness, because that's how I fell—"

"You didn't sing the lines into a new advance?" Fallows asked. His face looked lined and gray as he leaned forward.

"No, I didn't do that. But I made them wait to find out. I was so occupied with repartee and acting that I failed to seize the real chance of all the world. I told them I had been tried out as an anesthetic, but was not sure of myself in an opposite capacity. I begged them to send for the member of imperial orchestra stars—"

Poltneck's self-scorn was vitriolic as he now spoke.

"I told them I was a poor simple man afraid of great numbers, abased even before wounded, but that if they would wound the men first I would try. It was this that betrayed me—the joy of astonishing. Oh, they were without humor. It goes with the army—to be without humor. Really, you would have been dumfounded at the brittleness of mind which I encountered in the bomb-proof pit.... Of course, it had to come. It dawned on them—what I meant, and what the real state of my scorn was—at least, in part. And I was taken away, very pleased with myself and joyous—"

"I do not see where you failed. Where, where?" Berthe asked.

It was Fallows who understood first—even before Abel and Peter, who was not so imbued with the specific passion of the revolutionist.

"I was here—back in the city when it came to me what I might have done. And so clearly the cause of the failure was shown to me," Poltneck said, with a humility that touched Peter deeply, for his first thought had vanished before the fact that Poltneck neither in the action nor the narrative had once thought of his own life or death.

"I should have gone out to the lines and met the men face to face. Oh, it is hard—hard that I did not think of it, for I could have sung them home, instead of on into the valley. We might have been marching back now—all the lines crumbling—the bomb-proof pit squashed!"

The final stroke fell upon him this instant. None of the others had thought of it.

"And these—doors! Living God, we could have opened these doors!"

Their hands went out to him.

Chapter 3

A basket of food was sent in during the early afternoon. They gathered about, making a place for the woman under the light. Abel was brighter, his eyes full of tenderness. Poltneck had not long been able to hold out in his misery against the philosophy of Fallows, who said as they broke the bread:

"We have spoken our testimony, and the big adventure is ahead. It's against the law to look back. We are honored men. I am proud to be here, proud of a service that requires no herald. In all my dreaming in the little cabin in the Bosks I could think of no rarer thing than this—five together, a singer, a poet, a peasant, and two lovers. It's like a pastoral— but the dark suffering army is about us. ... Listen to the fighting. ... But there will be an end to fighting? ... Our Poltneck may already have sung the song to turn the armies back. Be very sure, he would have thought of his *coup* in time to-day, had the hour struck for that. Sing to us now, my son. Your soul will come home to you. Sing to us—*The Lord Is Mindful of His Own*—"

It was started as one would answer a question—food in his hand, and his eyes turned upward—a song of the Germans, too, the music of Mendelssohn.

... It became very clear to the five that the plan was good, that nothing mattered but the inner life, and that the soul breathes deeply and comes into its own immortal health, by man's thought and service to his brother. They saw it again— that goodly rock of things. The light was shining above. Their eyes filled with tears, and their hands touched each others' like children in a strange hush and shadow. ...

Will Levington Comfort

They heard a ragged volley of platoon fire from the distant court, but it did not hold their thoughts from the song nor change a note. The huge sandy head was turned upward, and the hand with its bit of broken bread moved to and fro. ...

Chapter 4

Boylan went back to headquarters again, but his nerve was breaking. He did not feel at one with the staff this afternoon, rather as a stranger who wanted something which the great brute force was unwilling to give. He was full of fears and disorders, as if all the eyes of men were searching his secret places. He told the sentry that he would like to see Lieutenant Dabnitz, and gave his name, much as a trooper would. He sat cold and breathing hard for many minutes—an outsider, as never before. Dabnitz came at last. Big Belt arose and clutched his arms.

"Lieutenant," he said. "I'll spend my life to prove you wrong about Peter Mowbray. I'll get the United States of America to thank you and General Kohlvihr, and the army for your kindness—if you spare him. I don't care to go to him—unless I can take him word. My God, Lieutenant, you mustn't shoot that boy! We've ridden together, all three. There's so much death without that. He's innocent as a babe of any revolutionary principle. I'll give America the greatest Russian story that—"

"My dear Boylan, believe me, you are wrong. They are deep as hell against us. You need not trouble, for they are happy as children at a birthday party—with Poltneck singing and all joined hands—"

Boylan's knees bent to the seat.

"But we will not disturb them for the time. We will let you know," said Dabnitz. "It would be a shame to interrupt such a pleasant party. Judenbach will be our headquarters for one more night."

Chapter 5

Moritz Abel was saying:

"... There is one perfect story in the world. It will bear the deepest scrutiny of mind or matter or soul. Physically it is exact; mentally it balances; spiritually it is the ultimate lesson. You will find in it all that you need to know about Christianity, for it is the soul of that; the one thing that was not in the world before the Christ came. You will learn in it who is your Father; who your Brother is, and who your Neighbor.

"It will impart to you the clear eye for shams and material offices and for the peril of fancied chosen peoples. From it you will draw the cosmic simplicity of good actions, and a fresh and kindling hatred for the human animal of grotesque desire."

"Children grasp it with thrilling comprehension; it silences the critical faculty of the intellectuals and animates the saint to tears of ecstasy, even to martyrdoms. It expresses the dream of peace alike for nations and men. It is a globe. You can go it blind, and win—following the spirit of the Good Samaritan."

Chapter 6

The light was gray that came down through the skylight. Abel and Poltneck and Fallows sat on the floor in the front end, because there were not chairs for all. Back in the shadows sat Berthe and Peter.

"...I think we will be a little bewildered," she was saying, "as one awakening from a dream, as one awakening in the sunlight. One stirs, you know, and shuts the eyes again. The reality dawns slowly—if the house is quiet.... It will be very quiet. We have been used to the cannonading so long, and the cries in the night. It will take us a moment to realize that it is all over. I think I see just how it will be then. I will have that sense of the glad unknown—that something long anticipated is about to happen. You know how it comes to one upon awakening, when something perfect is to happen—the presence of it, before one remembers just what it is?"

Peter nodded in the shadow.

"And then I will remember. It will be you. I will really open my eyes—and you will be there!"

Something of her fire came to him.

"You are sure it will be like that—afterward?" he repeated.

Her voice and lips trembled. "You ask just like a little child, Peter. It is the little child in you that strikes the heart. Don't you really believe in the *afterward?*"

"Yes, but I can't see it quite clearly, you know, as you do."

"You don't think it is all wayward and stupidly arranged as

Will Levington Comfort

the army would like to do it—do you?"

They laughed softly together, but she wanted him to see it, as she did, "Because," she said, "if you do, we will be together more quickly. I would have to go and find you, if you didn't come—"

"I should want to come," said Peter.

He followed her eyes beyond the twilight from the roof, to the face of Fallows, seen indistinctly in the shadows. It was like the figure of a Hindu holy man sitting there so low, his hands raised palms upward, his voice just audible.

"Listen," she said, her hand falling upon Peter's.

"It isn't so much their death that is the great wrong to the soldiers by the Fatherland. A man may do worse than die, at any time. It's the death of hate the Fatherland inspires—the fighting death—the going-down with blood-madness and hatred for the men of another country—not enemies at all, no harm exchanged whatsoever between them. It is such deaths that make the world hard to breathe in—the death of preying animals. But all that is passing. These battles had to come at the last to hurry it away...."

"That's what I wanted to say, Peter," Berthe whispered eagerly.... "Fallows is greater than any,—an inspirer. He will go out with his dream for men, strong and bright. Do you think that is the same as dying the fighting death—with a curse and a passion for the death of men whom you have never seen face to face?"

"It's quite all right, you know," said Peter. "I'm keen enough to see it through, but it's a closed door yet. However, there's something deathless about a woman like you—yes, I'm sure of that—"

Her hands pressed his swiftly. "Then you may be very sure, there's something deathless in the man she loves.... Listen, Fallows is talking about your country now:"

"... Russia is the invader, but America is the temple of the new spirit. America must reanimate the world after this war. I believe she is being born again now.... She was bred right. There is always that to fall back upon. She was founded upon the principles of liberty and service to the distressed. No other nation can say that. But America must lose the love of self, must cease to be a national soul and become the nucleus of the world soul of the future. Otherwise all that was holy in her conception is dead, and the passion of her prophets is without avail."

"There is a time for the development of the national soul, but ahead on the road is the world soul, the true Fatherland. The precious whisper is abroad that more sins have been committed in the name of patriotism than any other. The time will come when this little orbit and its slaying delusions will be well back among the provincialisms; not a bad word in itself, rather a lost meaning through abuse."

"Over a century ago the inspired Fichte addressed the Germans in a series of documents charged with the most exalted enthusiasm for the future of his people, on the basis of such a Fatherland that the only living answer could be the superb affiliation of men. For years and decades the gleam of that spiritual ignition endured there. Carlyle, not a country-man, saw it and made it blaze with the fuel of his genius. It seems dead to Prussia now, but that gleam shall never die. Some strong youth on the road to Damascus shall be struck to the ground by its radiance and arise to carry the light to the Gentiles.

"There must be such a voice in America now. I seem to feel the new genius of America, not yet in its prime, hardly articulate as yet, but rapidly maturing in these days of unparalleled suffering. They will interpret the New Age. They will meet the New Russia face to face. I think they are watching for us now. The bond is thicker than blood. They will see the future of Europe written upon these millions, now the invaders from the cold lands of poverty. I think they will hold the spirit until we come."

"All that was true of Germany when Fichte addressed his countrymen is true of America in this hour. All the physical and spiritual pressures of the European disruption are turned upon the temple of America to drive out the money-changers and make it the house of God."

Fallows' voice softened. He was talking of America with the passion of an exile. He loved the thoughts of her good, as he loved the peasants about him. The room was still.

"It is a time for heroics," he added. "America is emancipating her genius, not only from herself, but from the thrall of the old world's decadence. Do you think there is nothing fateful in the destructive energy that is rubbing out ancient landmarks? Rather it would seem that the old and the unclean has played its part, and may not be used in the new spiritual experiment. I want to hear America's new song—the song of the New Age—the unspoiled workmen at their task. They will sing as they lift.... Yes, we shall hear the song of the New Age. Since the pilgrims sang together, no such thrilling harmony shall move that western land. They shall be singing it for Russia when we come."

"It makes me so ashamed," Berthe whispered after a moment, "when I think of my weakness to-day, when you came. But, Peter, oh, I didn't want you to come—"

"I wouldn't be ashamed," he said. "It gave me something from you that I couldn't have had without it. There was plenty to hold a man in wonder—your zeal to do for others, and the exaltations, but to-day you were down in my valley, in the earth bottoms, just seeing in the human light, your wings tired. It was the best moment of the pilgrimage, Berthe—the deepest."

Peter had wanted to tell her that.

Chapter 7

Big Belt stood before a man of his own size—Lornievitch, the Commander of commanders, Himself.

It was night. Boylan had plunged into a new vat of power, and persuaded Dabnitz to furnish an escort from Judenbach, four miles to the east to the main headquarters of the Galician army.

Rows of sleepy stenographers in the outer room of a broad shepherd's house in a little hill village—a web of wires on the low ceiling, lanterns, candles, field 'phones and telegraph tickers, none altogether subsided; as much routine as in the management of a state—the center of this monster battle-line—to say nothing of the spectacular.

The two men now filled a small inner room. Lornievitch spoke English—an English much to the caller's liking. Perhaps it was the bond of bulk between them.

"Well, and so you are Boylan of the *Rhodes?*—what is it, Mr. Boylan? We are very busy."

"I have a young friend of *The States*" he began and talked for three minutes—talked until Lornievitch squirmed and his aides hurried forward ready to assist.

"And what does Kohlvihr say?"

"I had to speak to him through an interpreter. I could not get the answer I wanted. He has had a terrible day. The life of one American is too small for discussion there—"

"And you have come here to me. Meanwhile, on the wire is

the young man's case—a love affair with a revolutionist—
and a sort of be-damned to the Russian army. You are a
strong man, doubtless a brave one—"

Boylan was fighting for Peter's life as he would not have
fought for his own; and yet he warmed to the commander—
fibers all through him warming—something of man-business
about this office that made the headquarters at Judenbach
look sinister and den-like. It was just his hope in all
likelihood.

"But Mr. Boylan," Lornievitch added, "what would you do in
my case? There's big action, front, side, within. They have a
case against the others—and he is one of them."

"He may be one in a momentary infatuation—"

"Nonsense, Boylan—this is no time for girls!"

"I grant you that, sir. But he is not a revolutionist. I've slept
and ridden with him night and day. His paper wouldn't pay
for cigarettes to do other than tell the story from the army
end. If he's gone *loco*, I'll take him home under my arm—"

"I say, Boylan, what do you want of him this way? He's a
newspaper competitor—"

"Mowbray got to me. Didn't try to, but he's there. Took the
field as if it had been his work always. He's a friend, clever,
courageous, a gentleman always, clean cut, a laugh, a hand—
and a boy over it all. I didn't know—until I found him in
danger. I couldn't feel worse if I were his old woman—I am
twice his age, damn near—"

"You're invincible, Boylan. I'll tell you this: I feel better.
That's worth something. Things look black here in the

valleys. Something human I needed, in your coming. Go back now. Nothing will be done until the morning. We've had to shoot Austrian spies all day. Caught 'em red-handed. I feel red-handed, too. Go back, and before to-morrow morning I'll get an order over to straighten him out from the others—before final action is taken. Maybe I'll look him over myself. Good night.... Oh, I say, Mr. Boylan—"

"Yes, General."

"Oh, it doesn't matter. I was just thinking I'd like to have one friend like young what's-his-name of *The States* has—"

"Mowbray—Mowbray—don't forget the name, General—"

"Good-night."

"Good-night."

Boylan put his soul in it. He loved the Russians. It was far this side of midnight, but he smelled the dawn.

Back in his own quarters, as he yawned largely at the flickering shadows of the freshly-lit candle, he noted Peter's saddle bags on the floor, and considered that it might be well to get them over to-night.

Chapter 8

Peter walked the room, a changing star or two in the windy skylight; a candle in the center by the stair-door where the sentry stood; Berthe watching him steadily from her chair. The others at the far end looked up occasionally. They were talking low-toned. Poltneck had been singing folk-songs— pure spirit of the boat and cradle, of the march and the marriage and the harvest, of the cruel winter and the pregnant warmth again; songs that had come up from the soil and stream and the simple heart of man, older than Mother Moscow, old beyond any human name to attach to them. True and anonymous, these songs. The lips that first sung them never knew that they had breathed the basic gospel which does not die, but moves from house to house around the world. Indeed, the melodies were born of the land and the sky, like the mist that rises from the earth when the yellow sun comes up from the south, and the "green noise" of spring breaks the iron cold.

The moment had come when Peter could not sit still. Berthe was never so dear, but he could not stay. He held the three men in true full comrade spirit, but he could not sit with them now. He had nothing to fear; all was quite well.

He was thinking of America, that she was "bred right"; that some change might be upon her now, something akin to his own transformation. Was there a bond thicker than blood between America and the New Russia? Word had reached the field that Russia had put away her greatest devil in a day. A nation is to be reckoned with that makes her changes thus at a sweep. Had Russia not freed fifty million slaves at one stroke of the pen—that great emancipation of Alexander? And Russia now held the Earth's mighty energy of fecundity—an ultimate significance here; for this guest invariably

Will Levington Comfort

comes before a people has reached its meridian, and not afterward.... His companions of the death cell were touching the truth; this dark suffering army was the Europe of the future—the Russian voice that would challenge America to answer brother to brother.

The folk songs were singing in his soul, and the lines of Abel's *We Are Free,* the friendships of Spenski and Samarc, of these in the room, and the love of Berthe Wyndham.

All had prevailed. The culmination was now. He thought of the actuality of to-morrow, but without terror, or blankness. It would seem that he were leaving all this; that America, Russia, friendship, the love of woman, were no longer his portion; yet he seemed closer than ever to them. It was as Fallows said, "These things are immortal." Perhaps this very room, and this, the greatest of his days in the world, would be pictured by some one to come, as clearly and as magically as he saw it all now; by some young workman of the reconstruction, after the red horse of war was driven back forever.

He was sustained. The sense came clearly that nothing men might do could cause him harm. He felt even that his mother would some time know how well he had come to understand her at the last. Everything was answered by the mystic future. It was all there; all would be told.

"Why, to-morrow," he exclaimed aloud suddenly, "why, to-morrow, we will laugh at today."

They were about him. They seemed to understand all that had brought his words, as if they had followed his thoughts to the same apostrophe. ...He was laughing in the midst of them.

"I think it must have been the singing and all," he said breathlessly. "It got away from me. It has all been too fine to-day. I don't see—I really don't—how I managed to earn it all."

A step upon the stair, slow and heavy, a step that Peter Mowbray knew. The companion sentry had remained below at the street door, and now called to his fellow of the guard to open. ...Peter was abashed before his friend like a child that had disobeyed, and come to believe that he knew better than the father. It was Big Belt at midnight.

"I brought your shaving-tackle," he said. "Hello, Peter."

The face in the thin ray looked like polished metal.

"Come in." Peter had him by the hand, which was easily pulled across the threshold, but the body didn't move."

"No, I won't come in—"

"Boylan, come in!... I want you to meet—"

"No. I'll see you in the morning.... For God's sake, don't look so happy, and keep your mouth shut.... Good-night."

A curtain had fallen before the glowing future. Peter couldn't raise it again. He tried to restore his laugh and light-heartedness for the others, but it was a mockery. The world had come in all its chaos and mad fatigue. All that he had said was without meaning. The singing was over. Berthe gave him her hand as he returned to the dark corner. She did not speak, for a moment, and then only to say:

"How sensitive we are!"

All the weariness that he had ever known came upon him, gathering together for descent, pressing out vitality, leaving him cold and undone.

"You are very tired," she whispered. "Perhaps we can rest a little. The three are resting." Then a little later, like a child half-asleep, she added, "I love you."

It was her good-night.

Throughout that short night he dreamed of cedar boughs and pungent autumn air; flurries of snow falling from wide pine branches. There was gray in the skylight when he awoke. Berthe was near, her cheek against his saddle bags, which he had placed for her the last thing. Very white and small her face looked as she slept, her hands folded under her chin.... Peter watched, his eyes becoming accustomed to the faint light. The white cap lay near, a different and imperfect white compared to her flesh; and the soft deep night of her hair seemed to him of sufficient loveliness for any world. A girl asleep—and such a faith had they known. There was a beauty about it all that rebuked the actuality of the place and the town and the soldiery.

Misery began deep in his heart, welled up to his throat, blurring his eyes, resolving his whole nature almost past resistance; that a love-woman still without her chance, without her child, so fair and unafraid, who had asked so little for herself and so much for the world—should be brought to the shame and the shot of fools. A flutter of eyes. Mowbray gripped his self-control with every ounce of force. He would hold her in his power of will while she met the issue of the day, and its first cruel thought. Her brow contracted a little, as if through some passing pain.... The dawn of a smile that pursed her lips to speak his name, met his kiss instead. He held her face between his hands, smiling at her, while the realization came.

"Dear Peter—it's the day of our journey—"

He brushed the lather in gratefully with cold water. The touch of the razor gave him a queer pang such as he had never met before.

"You're just a boy," Berthe remarked.... "It must make one feel clean. It has been years since I was present—"

The others were now awake. They made merry over the shaving, all taking turns, even Fallows, the last and the longest. Indeed he had scarcely finished before their first test came. It was like a whip—that step upon the stair, but only a sentry with tea and bread.

Chapter 9

A gray dawn, an east wind with a driving mist, a miserable day afield in every promise, and Big Belt had missed none of these portents since the full darkness. With the first relief of the morning-guard at headquarters, he was there. Dabnitz appeared and smiled grimly. The wire was already busy; Kohlvihr came in unsteadily, the old fume about him that made Boylan lick his lips. His own nerves had been badly wrenched. He could have relished a stimulant, but he hadn't thought of it alone.

"You're looking for word from the Commander?" Dabnitz asked.

"Yes."

"So are we. It's up to him to-day. We're a mere wisp of what we were—"

Boylan simulated interest. There was but one idea in his world, however.

"By the way," Dabnitz added. "The Commander asked for full particulars this morning at three. They were sent to him—Mr. Mowbray's case—"

Boylan jerked up his chin. Of late, his woolen collar had apparently shrunk.

"You haven't heard yet?"

"Not yet. We're waiting—"

"Nothing will be done until you hear?"

"Not in Mowbray's case. The others—the others have had tea.... They are very quiet this morning—no singing."

Boylan hated him for that, a momentary but scarring hatred.... The field telephone began. Presently it occupied the steady swift attention of a stenographer whose pages were put on the machine and handed in strips to the staff members, like a last-minute news story to compositors. ...One of the hardest things Boylan ever did was to speak to Dabnitz as follows: "I'd better be there if you take the others and leave—leave Peter Mowbray. He's impulsive. You wouldn't want a scene—you know—"

"Wait a minute—I think your matter is on the wire," Dabnitz said, drawing back to the telegraph.

"Yes," he nodded, and a moment later handed Big Belt this message:

"My compliments to Mr. Boylan and assurances of excellent regard. I have found the favor he asks, however, altogether out of my power to grant."

Boylan's jaw dropped; his mouth filled with saliva. Dabnitz said something, "...desperately sorry... couldn't possibly have ended another way."

"Come, come—this won't do," Big Belt muttered queerly. He was not answering Dabnitz, but commanding himself.... He swallowed again and turned:

"You will have charge of the affair?"

"Yes, doubtless. It will be very short—"

"I will wait for you below. Of course, I'll want to be there, you know—"

"I didn't know," Dabnitz sighed.

Boylan was standing below. He heard distant firing through the rain in the direction of the field.... Lornievitch had doubtless begun a flank movement. Kohlvihr would lick his wounds in Judenbach for another day.

Dabnitz appeared from the stairway, a paper in his hand. He dispatched a sentry to the barracks for a platoon, and stood waiting impatiently for its coming. Big Belt, in the door of his quarters a few paces distant, swallowed again.... It might delay matters.... The black fact was that it would not do more....

"Oh, I say, Lieutenant, come here a moment, please. I want to show you something—"

Boylan led the Russian in, and turned. The place was empty. Dabnitz regarded him wearily—then with sudden amazement.

It was a kind of bear reaching. He was pulled down, his face smothered in a woolen shirt that covered a breast like cushioned stone. The building must have fallen. The hands were neither rough nor swift, but they pawed him with a kind of power that turned him to vapor. There was one finger upon his backbone at the neck that shut off the life currents.... Dabnitz opened his eyes presently—a choking wad of paper in his mouth. The mammoth looked down upon him and said:

"Excuse me, Lieutenant, but I had to have a chance to think."

At this instant Boylan saw the paper that the Russian had

carried. It had fluttered to the floor, Kohlvihr's signature in plain view. The weights that beset the American had now to do with the uselessness of it all. He had rendered the momentary order and its bearer ineffectual; he might possibly divert the platoon. But the great one-eyed system was all about, knowing its single task of destruction. It would turn back to that piece by piece—until the task was done. Yet while he lived, Boylan could not let it go on, in this specific instance. He was fighting the Russian army now; that die was cast; the one thing to do was to keep Peter Mowbray alive as long as possible. He went about further details without hope, however.

Dabnitz was carefully bound and lifted to the corner in the midst of saddles and kit. An extra strip was fastened around his chin to prevent the ejection of the gag. Big Belt spoke steadily and softly as he worked:

"You're a good soldier. You play your game to the seeds. I have no objection to you. When it's all over I'll think of you—as a corking field man. You've been good to us, too—everything you could do to make us comfortable and to help us see the wheels go round.... Only this one little thing. Perhaps you think I take it too seriously—this Mowbray thing. Perhaps I do. That's my funeral.... Wow, and I was merely speaking figuratively!... In any event I'm not a nihilist. I've only got Mowbray on the brain.... I've hurt you as little as possible. I won't leave you here long, my boy. I wasn't rough with you. You must have seen that—"

Dabnitz's eyes rolled.

"Well, you see I couldn't have a whole lot of noise. There's the true official timbre in your voice, Lieutenant.... Now you're snug, and the platoon is served in the street.... Look what's here! I'm a careless hand—six-shooter and belt. You'll rest more comfortably with 'em off. And a bit of a sword? I'll take that, too. ...I won't be long, Dabnitz."

He went forth carrying the paper. "Lieutenant was called to another task," he said haltingly to the enlisted officer in charge. "Hold your men here, until I come—"

The firing was intense valleyward. Boylan felt the need of thinking further and dashed into the headquarters' stairway. There were excited voices above, and he made haste to see. Kohlvihr was wild-eyed in the center of the upper room—the telegraph ticking nervously, half of his staff bending with extraordinary intensity over the birth of a certain message.... What they wanted came over the 'phone.

Boylan saw four Russian officers rush to the 'phone from the telegraph table.... Something had happened. He backed out.

"It's all off," he told the soldier. "Go back to barracks. The enemy has broken through—"

He wasn't sure of the last, but tore the paper and crumpled the pieces. The platoon reversed and vanished. At the far end of the street a cavalry squad was galloping forward, behind a single dispatch rider. Already the news was known in headquarters and the staff officers burst forth with orders for retreat—retreat to the eastward. It was no secret now. The enemy was crossing the valley that Kohlvihr had found impassable.

Big Belt felt the life brimming up in his heart. Then he thought of Dabnitz, and went to him, shutting the door behind.

"Do you *get* what's on, Lieutenant? Wink once—if you do."

Dabnitz shook his head.

"It's the enemy breaking through. Judenbach is to be abandoned *pronto*. Listen—"

The cavalry was in the street, carrying abroad the order for retreat.... They heard it plainly now, even the details. Hospitals not to be emptied, guns and ammunition not readily to be transported, must be destroyed. The final hell was started in the town.

"Dabnitz, I don't want you among the captured on my account. Just forget that order! The platoon has gone back. The staff is blocked and jammed with greater things. Will you forget it? Wink twice—"

There was no hesitation.

"Good. The sentries must be called off—that stair-door left open. I'll join them—and bother you no more. We'll not leave the room while the town changes hands. They'll never even ask you if that little job is done. Will you go with me now and do this? Wink twice—"

It was done emphatically; a beseeching for haste.

"Dabnitz, I trust you. I'll entertain you in America some time—all Washington and New York.... You'll do exactly what I ask—no more, no less? Good God, man, it wouldn't do any good to kill 'em now. They're out of hand forever. Perhaps the Austrians will do it, anyway. Wink twice—"

"Good." The gag was jerked free, and the various bindings.

"Now, come with me. I'll detain you but a second or two—"

Dabnitz walked at his side to the stair entrance of the skylight prison. He spoke to the sentry below. The officer of the guard was called; the sentry summoned from above, the door left open.

"Wait," Boylan said finally to Dabnitz. "Here's your gun, Lieutenant. I'm obliged to you. You'll know better some day what I mean by that—"

"Keep them under cover," Dabnitz said hoarsely. "I'll kill you or any of the others that I see in the street."

"You'd be quite right."

Dabnitz turned away. Big Belt deliberated. He did not quite trust the Russian. He had covered him with his little pocket gun, as he handed back the arms. Still Boylan couldn't have caused him to fall prisoner. His hope now was that the Lieutenant would find such a rush and turmoil that he would be compelled to forget the incident. ...He heard their voices at the upper door of the stairway.

"Is that you, Boylan?"

"Yep."

"Good-morning. What's up?" It was Peter.

"I haven't quite settled in my mind. You're not to come down. We haven't decorated the Christmas tree. I'm sentry here—"

The side street was deserted. The main highway was a throng, strange in its new direction of northward, for the bulk of energy had heretofore moved toward the valley. The sappers were at their work of destruction. The town rocked with explosions, but the main consideration to Big Belt was that moments passed without bringing further fighting to him, personally.

"Maybe he means to stick after all," he muttered. "He must see that I was square with him—"

Then Big Belt smiled grimly, as if he had heard his own words.

He watched with a kind of ferocity until the passing of the staff made him duck back into the doorway.... Kohlvihr sitting like a potato-bag, the brave but melancholy Doltmir— finally Dabnitz. The latter passed the little side-street without a turn of the head. After many moments Boylan ventured to the corner. Rifle shots from the southern border, and the smell of fire, were matters of critical interest. The main highway was all but emptied of Russians. One little party of artillerymen was struggling to save a big gun half-horsed. Three ambulances hurried by filled with wounded officers— but the cries of the thousands of wounded enlisted men went up from the hospitals which the Russians were abandoning. The lower half of the town was in a final ruin that blocked the streets.

But beyond as the wind cleared the smoke an instant (or the rain held it low to the earth), Big Belt saw a column of troops. Its single peculiarity struck him with queer emotion. He returned to the stair-door. A long-repressed volume came forth from his lungs, as he trudged wearily upward.

Will Levington Comfort

VI

THE FIELD OF HELMETS

Chapter 1

Peter turned back from the upper door, since nothing further in the way of news was to be had from Boylan. The first face that he saw within was Fallows', and over it, as his own glance sped quickly, there passed a look as from some poignant burden. It was the look of a man who had thought the fight won, and now perceived that it must be resumed again. Poltneck was just behind. Peter would like to have preserved in picture the singer's realization that the chance was life instead of death—the blend of animal and angel which is so thrillingly human, as it was expressed upon that countenance. Abel was smiling, something of a child in the smile, a tremulousness around the lips; and Berthe came forward under the rain-blurred skylight—gladness, animation, a touch of the great tension lingering, but something else that he had not seen before in their prison hours. He went to her.

"What does it mean?" she whispered.

"It means that the door is open, the sentries gone. Big Belt is below and the town wild with some new trouble—"

"The Austrians must have broken through," said Fallows.

"We are to stay until he gives us word," Peter added.

Berthe was leading him back to the shadows.

"Peter, does it mean that?"

He saw the dark low-glowing jewel in her eyes—the earth-shine, all the sweetness of earth in it. So close to death, it had not been ignited before in the skylight prison, but it was there for him now, and he loved her bewilderingly.

"I think we may almost dare to hope," he whispered.

"The still snowy woods—only a brave bird or two remaining —the short brilliant days and early nightfall—our talks that will never come to an end—"

Something of her longing frightened him—the danger of its intensity.

"I think we may almost dare to hope," he repeated.

"Peter, I think—I think you are braver than any—"

"Nonsense."

"But you did not *see* ahead! To you, it was a closed door yesterday and last night. Fallows wants to go. He's weary. Abel and Poltneck are old rebels with visions. They have thought much of such hours as we have known here. But you—I saw it the first day in Warsaw—the deadly courage. You had built no dream. You asked no future. You faced it—

light or black."

"Berthe—I almost broke this morning—when I looked at you sleeping—and last night after Boylan came.... I think I would have fought them in the street! It seemed—blasphemous for them to kill you—those dim fellows—"

"...Peter—"

She had seemed to lose her way, the light gone from her eyes, her lips cold.... A sprinkle of water, and she was smiling again in his arms.

"It's strong—too strong," she murmured vaguely.

The heavy step that Peter knew was upon the stairs. He listened. Yes, it was alone. Boylan appeared in the doorway.

"Go to him," Berthe whispered.

Peter obeyed. There was a gladness for him in the touch of the big hand.

"Tell us, Boylan," he said.

"They've gone."

"The Russians?"

"Yes."

Abel had propped a chair behind Big Belt, who sank into it eagerly.

"The Austrians have broken through?" Poltneck said.

"I'm not quite sure about that," Boylan answered. "The column I saw from the main road a minute ago—coming up from the valley—looked like *helmets* to me."

"Berthe, what did you mean by *'strong—too strong'?*"

Peter had stepped back to her for a moment.

"Did I say that?" she whispered smiling.

"Yes."

"I can't think of anything—but my love for you. It must have been that."

Chapter 2

For an hour in the skylight prison, they had waited for the step upon the stairs. When it came Fallows had an inspiration, and said softly:

"Sing to 'em, Poltneck—The Lord Is Mindful of His Own—!"

As before, the song was on the wing at the word.... Throughout the hour the Germans had flooded into the little city, the main column moving rapidly on in pursuit of the Russians, a comparatively small force remaining to garrison. As Boylan had pointed out, the new enemy must have appeared in tremendous numbers thus to dare such a drive through the Russian east wing. Lornievitch was at the head of a mighty force to the east; it was but the tip of the right wing that the Germans had cut off.

An old ranker had halted at the door, his platoon behind crowding the stairway. He was small and scarred, serious and decorous. Peter felt that the head under the helmet was shaven; that here was a man conscious of moving through the days of his life's stateliest fulfillment. Boylan was nearest; a little back from the rest Poltneck stood smiling, singing as he had never sung for the Little Father. It is a fact that the old ranker waited for the end of the stanza.
"Who are you?"

Peter talked: "Four of the hospital service from Warsaw, and two American correspondents, until to-day with the Russian army—"

The platoon-officer ordered his men at rest and sent for his Captain.

"Prisoners, you may sing," he said.

They heard the voices of the gathering in the street as Poltneck sang on, and presently the clatter of a sword in the stairway. A young officer, not the Captain, appeared. There was a quick appeal in the veteran's deference and his whisper. The old head bowed affectionately, too, as to a son of finer blood than he.

"Two American correspondents,—these two," he reported. "The others are of the hospital service of the enemy."

Poltneck had finished.

"Why are you here?" the officer asked.

"They were at work all night," said Peter, "and were here for a little rest. The change this morning was effected before they were aware. We were helping.

"You were helping?" the officer repeated.

"There has been much to do in the hospitals. We have been in Judenbach—this is the fourth day."

"We will look at your passports—yours and this gentleman's—"

The papers were produced. It was almost like a hand that came to Peter at this instant, though Berthe had not moved— the premonition that they were to be separated. He had planned nothing for this moment although it had been inevitable. There was a certain guilelessness about their whole presence together in the skylight prison, although Peter had tortured the facts a little—to avoid complication of making known their revolutionary parts. He had become so identified with his new friends, in the past three whelming days, that he had forgotten for the moment the great difference in his position as an American correspondent and noncombatant from Berthe's and the others.

Boylan had never forgotten. He had cursed his own slowness as a linguist, when Peter had taken the part of answering the German officer. He was afraid of Peter's answers, but that fear was passing now. In fact, Peter had answered surprisingly well, and his companion was breathing easily, as a man should in a state of mental health.

It was not until this moment—the German officer examining his passports, the ranker studying the insignia upon his sleeve—that Peter met the disaster of the future. It suddenly appeared to him—that life apart from *these* was bleak and a nothingness. To be caught in the great war-machine again, even with the superb loyalty of Boylan at his hand, had the grimness of death to his soul. Already he felt the new mastery of Judenbach, the hard insensitiveness of it—the stone and iron of its nature, the ineffable cruelty of its meaning and morale....

"These seem to be very complete and satisfactory," the young officer reported presently. "I shall furnish an escort to accompany you and Mr.—"

"Boylan," said the voice of the Rhodes' Agency.

"—to our Colonel Ulrich in charge of the garrison. These papers will go with you of course."

Peter cleared his voice and said steadily: "We have long given up any hope of getting anything out as newspaper men. I, for one, would be very glad of employment in the hospitals with my friends here. There has been work for many more hands than could be spared—"

"We appreciate your sacrifice," said the officer, "perhaps *we* are not so short-handed for the care of wounded. We have already brought in men not dead whom the Russian orderlies missed on the field yesterday. I believe the abandoned hospitals in Judenbach will not suffer for the change of flags."

Peter had noted Boylan's face as the German spoke. It was slightly upturned and like bronze in its hardness, reminding him of the night before in the candle-light. It weakened him.... He glanced about the room as the officer finished. Everywhere he saw their silent urge to accept. Fallows came forward.

"Some time again, dear friend—we will work together. All is well with us—"

Abel seemed to smile; Poltneck gripped his hand, neither venturing to speak, nor did the moment require it, for they had all gone down to the gates of understanding together.... Berthe's hands were in his.

Boylan had arisen.

"Your escort is ready," the German said.

Peter turned from them, but Berthe's face was placed for all to see.... A little warmth, the mild pleasure of untried friendship, the good wish of one fellow-worker to another in passing—this was all that the watchers saw. Even Peter in his great passion could draw no further message from that white upturned face. But her hidden hands, held in his, gave him the very respiration of her soul.

Chapter 3

Big Belt was alone with his friend again, but Peter seemed merely the body of a man, not much use. They were kept very close by the Germans, and told frankly that they were to be sent as soon as possible to the big prison-hospital at Sondreig. Even German correspondents were not permitted afield. Judenbach was retained, but the Americans were drawn forth by the exigencies of service with Colonel Ulrich's force, and on the afternoon of the third day following the German entry, they looked back upon the little hill-town a last time. Though there had not been sound nor sight of Berthe nor the group around her, during the three days, Peter was different afield, as if he missed a certain personal identification with that obscure Galician settlement where so much had happened. He moved about as if there were something dead inside. His world had turned insane.

Those were the terrible days of November, and the two Americans were forgotten at length—as a pair of buttons on the German uniform, forgotten because they served and were not in the way. All that had *not* to do with Berthe Wyndham was black as the Prussian night to Mowbray's brain, but Big Belt was always by. He could not have managed except for that. There were days in which it appeared as if half the world were down and bleeding; the other half trying to lift, pulling at the edges of the fallen, as one half-stupefied would pull at a fallen body in a burning house.

At night through the silences between the cannon, sometimes over the hills through the cold rains, came to Peter Mowbray's ears the sounds of church-bells. Boylan did not always hear them. The German officers declared that there were no such sounds. Boylan's sack was filled with blood.

"If I ever get out of here," he said, "I'll write one story—one battle till I die—and I'll call it 'Vintage Fourteen'."

For he was sick of the spilled wine of men. And other armies were fighting in the vineyards of France—as were these in the piney hills of the ancient shepherd kings; and what a fertilizing it was for the manhandled lands of Europe— potash and phosphor and nitrogen in the perfect solution of the human blood.

More and more Boylan saw that Peter was queer.

"I can't think," the latter would say. "I feel like a man dying, under a mountain of dead. Mostly I don't want to live. I don't want to die. I believe that it's all one and that this is the end of the world."

Peter could work, however. Day and night when they would let him, and mostly the Germans accepted his services gratefully now, he tugged at the dead and the dying in the field and in the field hospitals. And with the lanterns at night, often under fire, often so long that Boylan could not rest, but would wait at the hospital-division like a mother for a dissipated son.

"They call this the great German fighting machine," Peter whispered to Boylan one night, "but we're inside. We can't call it that. It's the most pitiful and devitalized thing that ever ran up and down the earth. And it doesn't mean anything. It's all waste—like a great body killing itself piece by piece—all waste and death."

He tried to make death easy for a soldier here and there, but there was so much. His clothing smelled of death; and one morning before the smoke fell, he watched the sun shining upon the pine-clad hills. That moment the thought held him that the pine trees were immortal, and men just the dung of the earth.

...One night Boylan asked as they lay down:

"Who are you?"

"Peter Mowbray."

"Yep, and I'm Boylan. You're at liberty to correct if wrong. Are we ever going to die or get out?"

"I don't know.... Boylan, you've been good to me. We're two to make one—eye to eye—"

"You're making a noise like breaking down again. Don't, Peter. I've gone on a bluff all my life. I'm a rotten sentimentalist at heart—soft as smashed grapes. It's my devil. If you break down, I'll show him to you—"

"It wouldn't hurt you to bellow like a girl."

"Maybe not, but I'd shoot my head off first."

"Did you see the old leprous peasant to-day? He was humpbacked, and he had no lips, but teeth like a dog. He pulled at a soldier's stirrup as we came into town. The soldier was afraid and shot him through the mouth—"

"Shut up, Peter, or you'll get me. I've shown you more now than any living soul knows—"

"You ought to show it to a woman. A man isn't right until a woman knows him in and out."

"For the love of God—go to sleep!"

They sank into restless death-ridden dreaming; and so it was many nights, until the dawn that they fronted a swift river, black from its snowy banks, saw the rising pine hills opposite and were swept possibly by mistake into the center of comprehensible action—a picture lifted from the hundred-mile ruck.

A little town, so far nameless, sat with a shivering look on the slope, about a half mile up from the river. A Russian quick-fire gun or two was emplaced in that vicinity, and two batteries of bigger bores (that the correspondents knew of) were higher on either side. Infantry intrenchments that looked like mole tracks from the distance corrugated the slopes in lateral lines, and roads came down to the two bridges that spanned the swift stream, less than a mile apart.

The morning was spent in artillery dueling. The Russians seemed partly silenced at noon. At no time was their attack cocky and confident. The Germans determined to cross in the early afternoon. This movement was not answered by excessive firing. German cavalry and small guns on the east bridge, a heavy field of helmets took the west. Boylan and Mowbray rode with the artillery. Even as the German forces combined for position, the firing of the Russians was not spiteful. There seemed a note of complaint and hysteria. There was no tension in the German command; it was too weathered for that.

Now the cavalry went into action and guns moved away farther to the east for higher emplacement.

"They're going to charge the horses up into the town. They haven't much respect for the infantry trenches," said Boylan.

At that instant Peter's mind opened a clearer series of pictures of Berthe Wyndham than he had known for days.

Palace Square near the river corner; her little house in Warsaw and the tall flowers between; across the siding after Fransic; her coming to the cot of Samarc, and all the wonderful films of the skylight prison—the dearest of all as she slept. He could not hold the battle in mind, for he was very rich with these pictures, and for days had tried vainly to think just how she looked. It had been easier to remember something which Peter designated secretly as her soul.

Suddenly the turf rocked under his feet and his body was bent in the terrific concussion from behind. They turned and saw the middle stone abutment of the nearer bridge lifted from the stream—the whole background sky black with dust and rock. Then, just as he thought of it, the west bridge went. He spoke before Boylan, and rather unerringly, as one does at times coming up from a dream.

"They've trapped what they think they can handle—and fired the bridges by wire."

Boylan said: "I can't call it German stupidity, because it didn't occur to me that the bridges were mined.... It's to be another leisure spraying. We're in the slaughter-pen.... God, man, look at the horses!"

It had been too late to call back the cavalry. Peter's eyes followed Boylan's sweeping arm. The horsemen were in skirmish on the slope, just breaking out into charge. The town above and the emplacements adjoining which had kept their secret so well, were now in a blur of sulphur and action directed upon the cavalry charge. The whole line went down in the deluge—suddenly vanished under the hideous blat of the machines—whole rows rubbed into the earth—a few beasts rising empty, shaking themselves and tumbling back, no riders. Peter turned to the infantry in formation on the western slopes. The Russian fire was not lax now, not discouraged in the least, nor hysterical. It was cold-blooded murder in gluttonous quantity.

The Americans forgot themselves. Cavalry gone—they turned to the west and saw the poor men-beasts in rout. Even the infantry comprehended the trick, and felt something superhuman behind it. They rushed back toward the river— swift, ugly with white patches and unfordable, requiring a good swimmer.... The eyes of Boylan turned back to the Horse. He had always loved the cavalry, ridden with the cavalry always by preference. Peter was watching the river— the hands up from the center of the river....

They were alone, and now the Russian machines were on the German batteries not yet emplaced, none unlimbered. It was as if the wind carried them the spray from the sweeping fountains, turned from the horse to put out the guns. Peter was hit and down—hit again and the night slowly settled upon him, bringing the bells.

Will Levington Comfort

Chapter 4

Big Belt talked to himself in that blizzard of fire.

"He's hit—hit twice—but we can't go back to the Russians. They'll finish the lad. Dabnitz promised. The Germans can't rescue us, because the bridges are down. I've got to get him across the river—"

He knelt and swung the burden across his back. The firing was thinner, and the weight hurried his great legs down to the water.... Personally he would have waited for recapture. How he would have laughed at Lornievitch in that case. But this that he bore was under sentence of death in that camp. He regarded the river now, propping up his head under the burden. It was a swift devil of a stream, black from its winter borders and cold. He moved toward the broken bridge, hundreds of soldiers doing the same. But none of them bore a burden.

Now he was on the steep and slidy bank-the roar of the current in his ears, the roar of the guns behind. The stone abutments of the bridge still stood, but the huge beams of the upper frame-work were sprawled in the stream, the ends visible. A string of soldiers crawled along, toward the center of the current. There was a place in which they disappeared.... He took his position in the waiting line and heard the cries wrung from the throats of those in the crossing—from the paralyzing cold. Only a few succeeded. Boylan saw this, as he awaited his turn. A steady grim procession on this side, whispering, crowding—but a thin and straggling output on the far bank. Scenes enacting in the center of the current shook his heart—faces and arms against the black water, the struggles and the cries of men as they were whipped away.

Big Belt was in; no crawl for him. He walked the ten-inch beam with his burden, as it sank deeper and deeper toward the center. The ice of the water bit and tore at him. It was like a burn, too, but the paralysis was not that of fire. The chill wrestled with his consciousness, as he reached the depth of his waist; the current was bewildering in its pressures—like a woman clinging to his limbs, betraying him to an enemy. A mysterious force, this of a running river, for the body of man is not built for it, and man's mind is slow to learn the necessity of slow movements. The temptation to hasten is like the tug of demons. There is much to break the nerve—and yet nerve must remain king of every action.

Boylan may have learned the trick in other wanderings. His own weight and the weight of his burden helped his feet in the rapid runs of white water. He made his way deeper and deeper upon the slanting ten-inch piece, holding his consciousness steady against the penetrating stab of the cold as it rose higher and higher, against the dizzying swirl of the stream, and against the fact that the timber might be broken at the center. ...The man before him seemed to go to his knees, reaching down with his hands. Then the white-topped rush took him.... One must stand; one must have weight to stand. The beam sunk to the center now-the water to his heart; the man behind urging.... One soldier ahead crawled forth where three had been.

Boylan's fears were equalized now by the sudden dread of the man behind. If he slipped he would catch at Peter's body.

"Go slow—that's the trick!" he called. "Feel for your footing each time. It's there. I tell you it's there, man! We rise in a moment more—"

He felt the jointure with his feet—some renewal or stoppage of the timber. He halted, yelling at the man behind:

"Wait—something different! I'll get you through—"

It was the slight turn of the top timbers as they had reached the apex.

"It's the top of the bridge," he yelled above the boom of the current, "—a turn like the peak of a low roof. A slight turn to the right. Now the climb—"

He put it in Russian somehow, making the words clear. His intensity was almost madness to keep the other's hands off.

A shiver passed through his burden. The water had whipped Peter's limbs. An added call for steadiness, but a gladness about it, too, since he was not carrying the dead.... Upgrade now. The soldier behind had passed the turn safely and was following.

...It seemed that he had walked hours, A thousand or more German soldiers were lost even as he. Their faces in the dusk passed him—to and fro—hoarse questions. The gray chill dusk was all about, quite different from anything Big Belt had known. His clothing had warmed to him from great exertion. There was a line that caked and dampened again down his left thigh, like an artillery stripe, from Peter's wounds. Night came on, finding him without a command—a strange sort of abandonment, and a certain fear of being overtaken by a Russian party. The character of his fatigue brought back ancient memories, when he had looked death face to face and was afraid.

"Who are you?" someone piped sharply in German.

He had moved long through the dark toward a moving file of lights.

"Two American correspondents."

"What's that you carry?"

"The other one."

Peter heard this. It seemed that terrible hands had been tugging at his flesh for hours; yet he could not move, and lay upon a bed that swung and swayed and stumbled.

"Two American correspondents," the voice repeated.... "Search...."

Then Peter looked into the dazzle of a flashlight, and the familiar voice said:

"Yes, he's hard hit and heavy as hell.... Passports in hip pocket-handle him gently. ... Thanks, I'll take care of this man—unless you have a stretcher—"

"To whom were you formerly assigned?"

"To Colonel Ulrich. We were across the river when that trap was sprung this afternoon—"

"Just about wiped you fellows out, didn't they?... Passports right enough as far as I can see. Stay here, I'll try to get a conduct. I'm afraid there isn't any Colonel Ulrich—at least I am of that opinion...."

Peter was let down. It puzzled him a long time because the ground was still. The big hands eased. His familiar was beside him, however, wet and panting. Now Peter seemed to remember that he had messages to carry.

"There's no other way—I've got to get through the lines—"

Will Levington Comfort

"Quite right," Boylan answered.

"I don't want to fail. She wouldn't look twice at a man who failed—"

"Hell, child, sit still. She'd look twice if you failed a thousand times.... Hai, don't tear open a man's bridle arm. What is it?"

"He was hump-backed—no lips—teeth like a dog—and the trooper shot him through the mouth—"

"I know, but he's dead. His back is straight now—don't look any worse now than ten thousand others...."

For a long time all was bewilderment. He had been lifted and lost consciousness again in the wrenching of the hands. Then slowly he came back and eternity began as before, his bed swaying and straining. The familiar voice was near, the German ahead. Sentry after sentry was passed, and each time deadly waiting.... In snatches he understood that the voice always near was Boylan's, but as often forgot it again. Once he realized that Boylan was carrying him, but he could not hold it in mind.... Now he was sure that it was Boylan. He wished he could die from the cold. He recalled that the cold climbs to a man's heart and then lets him out in comfortable dreams.

"Hai, you!" he heard in the familiar tones. "I can't go any further. Send a stretcher or a wagon. Tell 'em two American correspondents are sitting out here—one with a bullet or two through his chest of drawers—"

The bed was sinking now.... Then he was dragged across the big man's lap, and the voice was saying:

"I never knew it to fail. The man who wins a woman gets the steel, when it's anywhere in the air, but bullets fly wide and knives curve about a lonely maverick who has lost all his heart winnings."

They found Boylan so, his jaw clenched, the huge scarred head bare and covered with night dew, but ready to talk. Across his legs, Mowbray lay, and still breathed.

Chapter 5

Some unique thing, Big Belt, that rock of a man, had found in Peter Mowbray. For seven days and nights, though broken with incredible fatigues (a yellow line of bone color showing across his face under the eyes), Boylan sat by in cars and ambulances until they reached Sondreig, the city of the women-folk, and a regular civilized bed. What he gave to Peter was clear; what he took from a man down, a woman's property at best, is harder to tell. Perhaps in the great strains and pressures of the campaigns, he had seen Peter inside, the mechanism and light effects appertaining, and found it true. It may be that Big Belt had never been quite sure that a man-soul could be true, and having found one, was ready to go the limit. This is only a hazard.

Peter didn't know. He was a lump—one little red lamp burning in that long house of a man—flickering at that, its color bad, its shadow monstrous. Everyone but Boylan declared he would die from that wound in his chest; and Boylan was right.

The Germans were good. They gave him a little room over an apothecary shop at the edge of the city, off one of the bullet-wards, so that the American would suffer from no lack that the hospital routine could furnish, and still not be denied the ministration of his friend. There were reasons, from the German standpoint, why it was well for Mowbray to have every chance for life. The Russian *coup* of the destroyed bridges, that lesser disaster, would some time be told. Boylan might be persuaded to tell the story to America without adjectives. This was not a very humane way to regard large kindness from saddened and maddened men, and Boylan did not linger over it.

The Order in Sondreig soothed. It was like a fine *morale* shown by troops in a pinch. The city was one spacious hospital, but orderly, the horizon smokeless, the distance free from the crash of guns. In fact, it seemed that the city must have prepared itself for a thousand years—as if waiting for its messiah. There was a glad quiet in the thronging streets that seemed to say, "It has come...."

When he found that Peter would live—all the pathological vortices past—Big Belt turned with strange joy to exterior activities. Of course, months would be required to make his companion a man again. There might remain a crimp in him that would last always, but Boylan was aware that a man's weakness may be made his strength, and that a life habit of care which comes from cushioning a wound often results in extraordinary development of the parts of strength.

The sight of women and children brought him gusts of emotion. In one evening hour, he followed a middle-aged woman who was leading a child through the faintly-lit streets; trailed the pair for a square or two through the soft snow, a sort of miracle in the picture to him, a heaven of gentleness and order. This was his first grand reaction from the field of strife—at least, from this campaign—and he was struck as never before with the main fact—how little a man really needs to live his life in brightness and calm. Such a sense of the emptiness of war-fields surged home to him that he was left a heretic in relation to all that had called him before. It did not occur to Boylan that this was wisdom; rather the pith of the emotion was to the effect that he was getting old.

The child's thin voice reached him in questionings, and the steady low tones of the woman. A man could ask little more of the world than to lead a child thus.... Perhaps they were poor. Boylan would have liked to fix that. It had to do with the whole inner ideal of the man to be a fixer of such things—to come home to a house of little ones in quantity and many women—a broad house of aunts, sisters and old women, a long broad table of all ages, the many problems resting on him—and one woman looking straight across.... She would know everything, and yet would advise with him—quiet discussions of policy regarding this one or that one, and the interposition of food....

He was perspiring. Always after a war or expedition he had perceived such matters more or less clearly, but not quite as now. Never before had he constructed his secret heaven with such durable substance.... He actually believed that the field would never call to him again. It had become like the fear of hunger that he had learned once for all. No more of that—no more of war. He had given everything to the field, and lost his broad board in the world-house. At least, he could find a door-step somewhere.

They were gone. He thought of his companion—the sense of summons that he seemed to have known always. He turned and walked back. The snow fell softly; the street lights were pleasant and warming with this bit of peace in the world, this little circle of life with men and women and children together.... As he neared the apothecary shop, his thoughts became rounder and rounder with what he had missed. He had taken the arc and lost the globe—a sorry old specimen of a man, if the truth were told, a career behind him designed to arouse the wildness of boys, but without appeal and very much to be discouraged by real men. Finally it occurred to him of the whole races of men who had *what he lacked*, yet were restless for the harshness and crudity of the earth.

"If they only knew what they have," he muttered. "I suppose they forget. Just as I forget between wars what hell is like.... I suppose they do forget, and read a man's stuff by their fires (ordering the kids to be quiet)... thinking that this war-man writing from the field is a great and lucky guy. I suppose they stop and think how things might have been different with them—had *they* taken to the open when the old call came.... *Ordering the kids to be quiet*—Good God—"

Whether it was the audacity of fatherhood that called this last into the world, or the face of the woman who had passed him—is not known. Enough that Big Belt forgot all his dreams. ...That white-skinned, wonder-eyed girl, the fire creature, twice seen in the bitter shadows of Judenbach!

She had looked into his face, as if she scarcely dared to trust her eyes, as if she, too, were not sure; and yet it had come over him like death that she was here for her own.... He tried to make himself believe that it was an illusion, just one of the queer jolts that come to a man when his thoughts are far off. But actualities rubbed this out. She was a prisoner of the Germans; probably had proved invaluable in the hospital service and had earned certain privileges; but it wouldn't do to let Peter fall into her clutches again; that meant revolution and death. They would make a dupe of him as before. It had nothing to do with peace and the outer world; it meant—

Boylan saw that he wanted Peter for his own. He wiped the sweat from under his hat.... He couldn't keep them apart; she would think out a way; a man can't wrestle with a woman.... The world was bleak and wide-open to disruption again. He climbed the stairs.

The wounded man was not awake. Boylan had objected from the first to his manner of breathing—too much in the throat, hardly a man-sized volume of air, the breathing of one who hadn't proper lung-room; but this was an old matter. He reflected on the various fatigues Mowbray had met with a smile, and the vitality which had finally pulled him loose from the cold clutch itself; standing him in stead through a journey so grisly that Boylan had not had the detachment so far to contemplate it from first to last. So he had been forced seriously to grant exceptions to the rule of chest inches and vitality. The soft winter air blew in from the slightly opened casement.

Peter's face was wan and boyish—different to Boylan as a result of his encounter in the street. He saw Peter now with the eyes of a man who must give up.... She was here in Sondreig. He would not help her, but if she came, there would be no fight.... It had been his fault. Boylan had sensed the danger of giving too much—from the beginning.... One woman brings a man into the world, sees him properly a man, and another woman takes him away.... Just how Big Belt broke into this particular picture must be suggested rather than explained. He was very close to mothers that night. He could understand fathers, too.

...They would never know what he had done. The Russians had not understood, except Lornievitch, in part, and he was far away; the Germans would never piece the fragments together, and Peter himself had been mainly unconscious. Peter had not been told even of the Dabnitz episode.... They might have pulled together for years if it hadn't been for the woman, but there was bound to be a woman. Mowbray was like that.

Big Belt yawned over it all, drew his cot close, so he could hear Peter's call, lit a fresh candle, and wished he had remembered to smoke outside. Presently, however, he was breathing forth the full volume of a man.

Sitting by the civilized bed early the next afternoon he heard a voice below that clenched his jaw much as it had been that night outside the German camp before the stretcher was brought. She had found them. She did not speak first, but looked in.... Seeing the face upon the bed, she could not ask, nor speak, but crossed the room. It would have been just the same so far—had Boylan not been there. In fact, he had withdrawn from the place by his companion.... She knelt an instant. Now she arose and faced the friend.

"He will live."

Peter was still afar off.

"Yes, ma'am—I think he will."

She came to him now. "I saw you last night," she whispered. "I saw you come here. I could not come until now."

"Humph—" or something of the sort was heard from Boylan.

Berthe appeared to draw a certain truth from the situation. Perhaps she saw *the woman* in Boylan—the mysterious, draggled creature which he designated his devil on occasion. The old war-wolf gave her credit for no such penetration. Still she kept herself second, advised, assisted for a few moments, but would not let Boylan go.

"He's knit to you. He might die if you go," she said.

Something about her choked him. He had been with men so continually.

"And then I can't stay," she whispered. "But I am so thankful to have found you—that nothing else matters.... You see, we are prisoners. They have trusted certain of us to work; still we have no names, no way of hearing, no mails, or anything. It's a good miracle that I found you."

Presently she said again: "You don't think I understand, but I do. You have stood by him. He would not have been here but for you. He is living because of you. I see that. I see that he has been very close.... You may hate me as you wish, but you cannot help taking what I give you."

"You're an all-right young woman," Big Belt managed to remark. "I knew something of that." Then, in a panic, he added: "He'll know you to-night. He's cool now. He'll pull through. He'll know you to-night, and then I go."

"Not until he sees you.... Besides, I am a prisoner. I cannot come and go as I would. I may not be able to come to-night—they may say *no*." "He'll have all that he needs until you come," Boylan said.

She did come that night. Peter had returned, but voyaged again meanwhile. In the morning she came again.... Boylan ordered her to sit down in the far corner. He went to the bed, for Peter was stirring, and presently opened his eyes with reason and organization in them.

"Hello," he said.

"Hello, boy."

Peter looked beyond him and around the room.

"Go to sleep," said Boylan.

"I won't."

"All right."

Big Belt stepped aside. Peter managed to get a knuckle up to rub his eyes.

"He's back with us," Boylan whispered.

"Don't go," she pleaded.

"Don't be a fool," said Boylan.

She was there beside him, bending lower and lower. It was against nature for them not to forget the exterior world for a moment, and Boylan was on the stairs....

He saw Sondreig with eyes that seemed to have dropped their scales. It was early in the morning, and a light snow had freshened everything. An old woman was sitting at the locked entrance of what had been a dairy shop, weeping for her only son. Boylan stopped.

She was very poor and weak.

"Come, mother," he said, lifting her.

She looked into his face in a way that roweled the man.

"Come on," he said softly. "We'll have some breakfast. And you'll tell me about it. I belong to the widows and the fatherless, too."

So they rocked away together.

Chapter 6

He was sleeping again. Berthe went to the window. Even in
her happiness she was afraid, for she was remaining longer
than her leave.... The window faced the south, and the
apothecary shop was on the edge of town. The day was like a
pearl—snowy distance, a soft-toned sky and the low shine of
the sun. Deep down in the west, like an island, was a thick
brush of cedars, preserving their green across the miles, and
calling to her with something of the native wonder of old
Mother Earth; and to the right, east of south, was the huge
blurred stockade where King Cholera was so far imprisoned
with the bait of fresh lives each day.

The old Mother was in her winter bloom, so pure and deep-
eyed, so calm and above sorrow in her distance and coloring,
that it became to Berthe a moment not to be forgotten—such
a moment as would make a woman homesick in heaven.

...If the big man would only come back. They might be angry
for her staying. It would be so easy to lose all that she had
won from the Germans. They had come to rely upon her
more and more, realizing the character of her service, and
forgetting its origin in Judenbach. She did not want to
disappoint them. With Peter Mowbray here in good hands
and climbing back to life—no woman in the midst of war
could ask more.... At the bedside again, she pondered the
recent weeks to this hour. Without words, without heaviness,
he had come along, fitting so blithely into the new places,
bringing his laugh and his skepticism of self always, asking
for no sign nor reward of the future, building no dream of
heaven, but standing true to the tasks of earth. Greatly more,
and differently, she loved him now, and the distance held the
green of cedars.

...An officer came to her from the bullet-ward.

"You are to stay until Mr. Boylan, the correspondent, comes," he said.

"But will they know? They were good to let me come."

"Colonel Hartz has signed the order. Word has been sent to the entrainment wards. You were attached there, I believe?"

"Yes."

"Let us know in case of any need here."

"Yes. Thank you."

Chapter 7

A most satisfying adventure, so that Big Belt added many things to the matters which could not be related. The old mother had told him of her son (as they sat together in the little room she called home) and Boylan had seen in him a singular hero, and made the mother see it. Presently he strode forth to the shops and returned with many packages of food affairs, and a cart of fuel following. The prodigious prices which these things commanded in Sondreig appealed to him as a trifle; in fact, the simplicity of life on these direct terms of living first hand, struck him as the eternally right way.... Then she cooked for him, very intent and eager in the great joy of it, agitated by his praise. In fact, he went to great lengths of breakfasting to show his appreciation; until, perceiving what he had done, he strode forth again with replenished understanding and restocked the cupboard by means of the cart.... Yes, he would come to-morrow.... Yes, by all means, while he was in Sondreig.

Even if he had not thought of the white-fire creature being held in the room above the apothecary shop for his return, Boylan had found it necessary to leave the old mother, since she could not be made to eat with him there. She would have cooked for him until she fell by the fire, but as for her sharing the repast, she begged him to have peace, that time was plentiful for that.... He was thinking it all out once more, a most delectable incident, as he walked swiftly through the snow toward the apothecary shop, when his shoulder was plucked by a passerby, and he turned, stiffening a bit at the roughness of it. A black-bearded man of much rank peered into his face, crying out:

"Boylan, by the One God!"

"Herr Hartz—by the same!" Big Belt exclaimed.

And now they embraced—a mighty affair, a memorable spectacle of pounding, of disengagement, of renewed embrace—so that soldiers and hospital men circled wide in passing, and the little street was hushed with the exceeding joy.

"Come and live with me, Boylan. I will not take no for an answer. Come at once, and let us a table between us have, to prevent further inderrupption of travvic—"

At no time would the cause of this majestic effusion have been made clear to an outsider, though it was plain that the American correspondent and the German officer of rank shared it alike. The truth: these two, and two others somewhere in the world, were the surviving four of a complement of over thirty men who had made up the original outfit now known as the Schmedding Polar Failure. Colonel Hartz, detached from his cavalry command for service in the prison-hospital at Sondreig, was second in command here as he had been to Schmedding in that former ill-starred expedition.

The table was between them.

"But first," said Boylan, "there is a little business in which you can help. My friend, Mowbray... is just coming back to life from Russian wounds. I could not leave him without being assured of his care. There is one little nurse from the entrainment wards—it is a good story, which I will tell in good time—competent to care for him. She is there now, but I have already stayed longer than her leave granted. She must be set at rest, and word sent also to her own post—"

"So much words for a little thing—dictate and I write. Then

tell me of yourself, which is more imbortant—"

It happened, even after the messages were sent, that Boylan spoke very little of himself. He was grappling with a certain final disposal. His talk was colored with desire. In fact, within an hour he had reached the critical part of his narrative, and was becoming more glib momentarily as the way out cleared:

"...You see, they met in Warsaw, where I was stationed before the war. She did not tell him what was in her mind. He parted from her—as any other married man taking the field. We were together with Kohlvihr's column, of which I will tell you later.... Now what do you think?"

Herr Hartz snorted. He did not care to think.

"She didn't stay in Warsaw," Boylan went on, with great intensity. "No, my friend, she joined the hospital corps, and followed him afield—"

"The Russians take anyone for the hosbittles," the other remarked impatiently.

"Exactly; and my friend Mowbray found her nursing sick soldiers in Judenbach. It happened that they were together when the city changed hands. By the way, there was much of interest in those days of which I will tell you later.... This is the point. She was a Polish prisoner—he an American non-combatant. I advised them to say nothing for the present that they were married. It was very ticklish to change hands anyway, and would have complicated the position of each one. So they were separated. He was with me day by day until he was wounded. He moved in a dream without her—a good boy, Colonel—and a good girl—but war. I say, we learned something about men, you and I—long ago—"

Herr Hartz now beamed.

"We learned it," he breathed.

"They make only a few on the pattern of Mowbray.... Last night I saw her in the street here at Sondreig.... So you see why I arranged for her to take my place at his side—but you can arrange the rest—"

"For God's sake, what do you want? You talk and talk about such people and women and love stories—when we have so much to say about ourselves—"

"Be patient. We have all time," said Big Belt. "I only want them together—a true married pair. Then they will be off my hands. You can make Headquarters forget she is Polish—that is all. Some little place apart—for them to be together while he heals—"

"Such a lot of talk for small things. It shall be done, Boylan, with a paper. I will send them to the country and monobolize you myself. This is a big war—yes?"

Chapter 8

A last time he climbed to the floor above the apothecary shop. If only she wouldn't act up. A serious thing, this he had done. Big Belt felt that he had rushed matters, possibly treading upon a host of delicate and incomprehensible affairs. But, when he had found in Colonel Hartz a man to make action of his words, he had plunged....

Peter was asleep. The woman came forward noiselessly, offering her hand. By her face he knew that all was well with the patient. Boylan had stiffened to resist the pang of Peter's passing from his life. This had so far prevented his voice from softening to the woman. It was now evening.

"I've done what seemed best," he began abruptly in a whisper. "It appears to have accomplished what I set out after, but it's likely a ruffian's way—"

Her gray eyes widened, her face blanched.

Big Belt cleared his throat. Whispering was difficult.

"I met an old friend who made possible your remaining here. He's to send you into the country—as soon as the young fellow is able to be moved. You are to take care of him there. You see, my friend happened to be second in command here at Sondreig, and he thinks he can make all concerned forget that you were picked up from the opposition in Judenbach—"

"Can make Sondreig forget that?" she whispered.

"We are very old friends. We were out together in a former service—"

"And we are to be sent into the country—as soon as Peter is able?"

"Yes."

"But what is the terrible part?"

"There might have been a better way, but I didn't think of it—"

"Oh, what, Mr. Boylan?"

"I told him that you two were married—"

"Yes."

"I say, I told him that you two were married—"

"Yes—and then?"

Big Belt backed from her, and sat down.

"There isn't any *then*," he said. "That's it.... That you were married in Warsaw, and followed him to the field—without his knowing."

"Is that all?"

"Yes, ma'am."

"Oh, you frightened me."

...Boylan was on the stairs. He halted, turned back. She came to him eagerly.

"But *were* you married?" he asked.

"No. But it's such a little thing compared to what might have happened—to keep us apart. I mean what might have happened here.... Oh, God bless you!"

He twisted his chin away from his collar, drew it clear with his hand, cleared his throat to speak, and vanished.

VII

THE GREEN OF CEDARS

It wasn't an open fire, but a little iron stove that got so red that it trembled, and at intervals could hardly contain the puttering of the pine; and there was a one-armed soldier, who spent the long forenoons cutting carefully and piling, until there was a rustic wainscot half around the room, the drying breath of which was the purest fragrance in the world.... They petted the soldier until an officer came down.

It was the hunting forest of a certain Count, and the hut they lived in was but the lodge of one of his keepers; but it was far enough from the great mansion (where wounded officers of royal blood and toppling rank healed or died in much the same fashion as other men) to afford the silence and solitude they had dreamed of. And all about them the great trees pondered between the winds—pine and balsam, cedar and fir. It had looked like a bit of an island from the Sondreig window, but proved a true forest when they reached there—an enchanted one to Berthe and Mowbray.

Twice Boylan came down for a day, bringing Moritz Abel the second time; but the Colonel, whose authority had done so much for them, required much of Big Belt, and there was a woman (some mystery about this) who would keep dinner waiting, he said. So both times he had started back while there remained light in the sky. And Peter had become thoughtful.

"Why, there are whole days I can't account for," he muttered. "He must have had me strapped to him for days at a time."

He had asked for Poltneck, of whom she had seen the last in Judenbach. The Germans had loved his singing and made very much of him; and Peter had asked for Moritz Abel before the latter came for the day. Berthe had answered freely, but of Duke Fallows she had not spoken in a way to satisfy his questions. In fact, it was not until the day that Peter first crossed the little room alone that she seemed ready to speak. That afternoon he had called her from the window.

"Where is Fallows, Berthe?"

"Not far from here," she said. "Not as far as Sondreig from here—a place you have never seen, but I watched it every day from the window of the apothecary shop until you were moved. He offered himself at once when he heard—the cholera quarantine.... But he left a message for you to carry, Peter—gave it to me for you.

"I saw him for a few brief moments after he had volunteered. He talked of you and that other American boy of the other war. He said that the night he separated from that other—just after the battle of Liaoyang, the Russians in full retreat, he had written his story of the battle—the story of the Ploughman, and intrusted it to his friend to carry to America. He wants you to carry his story of this service—asked me to give it to you when you were better—to take to America with yours. 'Just a picture,' he said. 'It may be all wrong, but I see it so to-night, and I would like to have it come out in America some time.'"

"He is very dear to us, Peter—that old burning exile. Some time we may understand his love for America.... It was hard to let him go. They fight day and night in the Stockade. They are trying to spare Sondreig.... I wish you might have been with him that last night before he went. It was before I found you—before I saw the big man in the street.... He was glad to go. There was no sense of sacrifice in it. His whole sense was of our sorrow and the world's sorrow. But it would have been good for him if you had been there—because you are of his country. He said it again and again: 'She must see it. It is her immortal opportunity,' meaning America—"

"Is his story so we can see it?" Peter asked.

"Yes."

She took from her breast a little chamois, in which was wrapped two pages of tough tissue, spread them out, drew her chair close to him, and read this picture Fallows had made, and his message to America:

...It is the long night of Europe. France sits in dust upon the ground, staring toward the End. Mother England has called for her sons, and some have not answered. She turns her frost-rimed glass from the grim horizons to the grimmer skies, and always in the movement of the darkened shadows is written the word, "Disaster." ...Smileless Germany, stricken as never a nation was stricken before, save by the wrath of God, still holds to the fatal enchantment of a fatherland of the ground, while the changes in the Prussian boundaries are marked in fire and the blood of her children.... Russia is looking southward, furious to open her casements upon the perilous seas—gloomy millions of the tundras, mighty millions of the ice-ringing plains—looking southward, marching southward, to-day marking time, to-morrow a league, but southward as a ship in passage. Russia, the young, holy genii battling with demons in her breast, everything to win and only the fruits of her world-shocking fecundity to lose—southward to slaughter through the long night.

...A call to America through the long night—the voice calling for her to put on her splendid, her initial magic. The voice from the vision of sorrow-illumined men in frozen bivouacs, crying to America to hold fast to the dream of her Founders, lest the vessel of the future be drained of vital essence, indeed—to hold fast until we come ...crying for America to answer, not with rapacious intellect, not the answer of a militant body, but an answer from the soul of the New World, with its original vitality in the Fatherhood of God.

...Repeating through the long night that the patience of Nature is exhausted with the hate of man for man; that the hatred of nation for nation is a lost experiment; that the bitter romance of the predatory is a story finished in hell; that the passion for self and boundary is done, that Compassion for neighbor and nation is the art of the future; crying the end of the national soul and the stroke of the hour for the birth of the world-soul; crying to America, the only temple, the sole house of nativity, to put on again her youthful magic, to ignite afresh the Gleam of her Founders, to arise to her superb and heroic destiny. They sat in silence until the tap at the door. It was the one-armed soldier, who came in, regarded the stove critically inside and out, judiciously chose one knot of pine, inserted it with grave care, and, departing, inquired if there was anything further he could do.

"No," said Peter.

And Berthe asked: "Is there anything we can do for you?"

He bowed his head in the doorway, and they saw beyond him the winding aisles of the forest—green and white, the dusk creeping in.

THE END

Will Levington Comfort

Choose from Thousands of 1stWorldLibrary Classics By

A. M. Barnard
Ada Leverson
Adolphus William Ward
Aesop
Agatha Christie
Alexander Aaronsohn
Alexander Kielland
Alexandre Dumas
Alfred Gatty
Alfred Ollivant
Alice Duer Miller
Alice Turner Curtis
Alice Dunbar
Allen Chapman
Alleyne Ireland
Ambrose Bierce
Amelia E. Barr
Amory H. Bradford
Andrew Lang
Andrew McFarland Davis
Andy Adams
Angela Brazil
Anna Alice Chapin
Anna Sewell
Annie Besant
Annie Hamilton Donnell
Annie Payson Call
Annie Roe Carr
Annonaymous
Anton Chekhov
Archibald Lee Fletcher
Arnold Bennett
Arthur C. Benson
Arthur Conan Doyle
Arthur M. Winfield
Arthur Ransome
Arthur Schnitzler
Arthur Train
Atticus
B.H. Baden-Powell
B. M. Bower
B. C. Chatterjee
Baroness Emmuska Orczy
Baroness Orczy
Basil King
Bayard Taylor
Ben Macomber
Bertha Muzzy Bower
Bjornstjerne Bjornson

Booth Tarkington
Boyd Cable
Bram Stoker
C. Collodi
C. E. Orr
C. M. Ingleby
Carolyn Wells
Catherine Parr Traill
Charles A. Eastman
Charles Amory Beach
Charles Dickens
Charles Dudley Warner
Charles Farrar Browne
Charles Ives
Charles Kingsley
Charles Klein
Charles Hanson Towne
Charles Lathrop Pack
Charles Romyn Dake
Charles Whibley
Charles Willing Beale
Charlotte M. Braeme
Charlotte M. Yonge
Charlotte Perkins Stetson
Clair W. Hayes
Clarence Day Jr.
Clarence E. Mulford
Clemence Housman
Confucius
Coningsby Dawson
Cornelis DeWitt Wilcox
Cyril Burleigh
D. H. Lawrence
Daniel Defoe
David Garnett
Dinah Craik
Don Carlos Janes
Donald Keyhoe
Dorothy Kilner
Dougan Clark
Douglas Fairbanks
E. Nesbit
E. P. Roe
E. Phillips Oppenheim
E. S. Brooks
Earl Barnes
Edgar Rice Burroughs
Edith Van Dyne
Edith Wharton

Edward Everett Hale
Edward J. O'Biren
Edward S. Ellis
Edwin L. Arnold
Eleanor Atkins
Eleanor Hallowell Abbott
Eliot Gregory
Elizabeth Gaskell
Elizabeth McCracken
Elizabeth Von Arnim
Ellem Key
Emerson Hough
Emilie F. Carlen
Emily Bronte
Emily Dickinson
Enid Bagnold
Enilor Macartney Lane
Erasmus W. Jones
Ernie Howard Pie
Ethel May Dell
Ethel Turner
Ethel Watts Mumford
Eugene Sue
Eugenie Foa
Eugene Wood
Eustace Hale Ball
Evelyn Everett-green
Everard Cotes
F. H. Cheley
F. J. Cross
F. Marion Crawford
Fannie E. Newberry
Federick Austin Ogg
Ferdinand Ossendowski
Fergus Hume
Florence A. Kilpatrick
Fremont B. Deering
Francis Bacon
Francis Darwin
Frances Hodgson Burnett
Frances Parkinson Keyes
Frank Gee Patchin
Frank Harris
Frank Jewett Mather
Frank L. Packard
Frank V. Webster
Frederic Stewart Isham
Frederick Trevor Hill
Frederick Winslow Taylor

Friedrich Kerst
Friedrich Nietzsche
Fyodor Dostoyevsky
G.A. Henty
G.K. Chesterton
Gabrielle E. Jackson
Garrett P. Serviss
Gaston Leroux
George A. Warren
George Ade
Geroge Bernard Shaw
George Cary Eggleston
George Durston
George Ebers
George Eliot
George Gissing
George MacDonald
George Meredith
George Orwell
George Sylvester Viereck
George Tucker
George W. Cable
George Wharton James
Gertrude Atherton
Gordon Casserly
Grace E. King
Grace Gallatin
Grace Greenwood
Grant Allen
Guillermo A. Sherwell
Gulielma Zollinger
Gustav Flaubert
H. A. Cody
H. B. Irving
H.C. Bailey
H. G. Wells
H. H. Munro
H. Irving Hancock
H. R. Naylor
H. Rider Haggard
H. W. C. Davis
Haldeman Julius
Hall Caine
Hamilton Wright Mabie
Hans Christian Andersen
Harold Avery
Harold McGrath
Harriet Beecher Stowe
Harry Castlemon
Harry Coghill
Harry Houidini

Hayden Carruth
Helent Hunt Jackson
Helen Nicolay
Hendrik Conscience
Hendy David Thoreau
Henri Barbusse
Henrik Ibsen
Henry Adams
Henry Ford
Henry Frost
Henry James
Henry Jones Ford
Henry Seton Merriman
Henry W Longfellow
Herbert A. Giles
Herbert Carter
Herbert N. Casson
Herman Hesse
Hildegard G. Frey
Homer
Honore De Balzac
Horace B. Day
Horace Walpole
Horatio Alger Jr.
Howard Pyle
Howard R. Garis
Hugh Lofting
Hugh Walpole
Humphry Ward
Ian Maclaren
Inez Haynes Gillmore
Irving Bacheller
Isabel Cecilia Williams
Isabel Hornibrook
Israel Abrahams
Ivan Turgenev
J.G.Austin
J. Henri Fabre
J. M. Barrie
J. M. Walsh
J. Macdonald Oxley
J. R. Miller
J. S. Fletcher
J. S. Knowles
J. Storer Clouston
J. W. Duffield
Jack London
Jacob Abbott
James Allen
James Andrews
James Baldwin

James Branch Cabell
James DeMille
James Joyce
James Lane Allen
James Lane Allen
James Oliver Curwood
James Oppenheim
James Otis
James R. Driscoll
Jane Abbott
Jane Austen
Jane L. Stewart
Janet Aldridge
Jens Peter Jacobsen
Jerome K. Jerome
Jessie Graham Flower
John Buchan
John Burroughs
John Cournos
John F. Kennedy
John Gay
John Glasworthy
John Habberton
John Joy Bell
John Kendrick Bangs
John Milton
John Philip Sousa
John Taintor Foote
Jonas Lauritz Idemil Lie
Jonathan Swift
Joseph A. Altsheler
Joseph Carey
Joseph Conrad
Joseph E. Badger Jr
Joseph Hergesheimer
Joseph Jacobs
Jules Vernes
Julian Hawthrone
Julie A Lippmann
Justin Huntly McCarthy
Kakuzo Okakura
Karle Wilson Baker
Kate Chopin
Kenneth Grahame
Kenneth McGaffey
Kate Langley Bosher
Kate Langley Bosher
Katherine Cecil Thurston
Katherine Stokes
L. A. Abbot
L. T. Meade

L. Frank Baum
Latta Griswold
Laura Dent Crane
Laura Lee Hope
Laurence Housman
Lawrence Beasley
Leo Tolstoy
Leonid Andreyev
Lewis Carroll
Lewis Sperry Chafer
Lilian Bell
Lloyd Osbourne
Louis Hughes
Louis Joseph Vance
Louis Tracy
Louisa May Alcott
Lucy Fitch Perkins
Lucy Maud Montgomery
Luther Benson
Lydia Miller Middleton
Lyndon Orr
M. Corvus
M. H. Adams
Margaret E. Sangster
Margret Howth
Margaret Vandercook
Margaret W. Hungerford
Margret Penrose
Maria Edgeworth
Maria Thompson Daviess
Mariano Azuela
Marion Polk Angellotti
Mark Overton
Mark Twain
Mary Austin
Mary Catherine Crowley
Mary Cole
Mary Hastings Bradley
Mary Roberts Rinehart
Mary Rowlandson
M. Wollstonecraft Shelley
Maud Lindsay
Max Beerbohm
Myra Kelly
Nathaniel Hawthrone
Nicolo Machiavelli
O. F. Walton
Oscar Wilde

Owen Johnson
P.G. Wodehouse
Paul and Mabel Thorne
Paul G. Tomlinson
Paul Severing
Percy Brebner
Percy Keese Fitzhugh
Peter B. Kyne
Plato
Quincy Allen
R. Derby Holmes
R. L. Stevenson
R. S. Ball
Rabindranath Tagore
Rahul Alvares
Ralph Bonehill
Ralph Henry Barbour
Ralph Victor
Ralph Waldo Emmerson
Rene Descartes
Ray Cummings
Rex Beach
Rex E. Beach
Richard Harding Davis
Richard Jefferies
Richard Le Gallienne
Robert Barr
Robert Frost
Robert Gordon Anderson
Robert L. Drake
Robert Lansing
Robert Lynd
Robert Michael Ballantyne
Robert W. Chambers
Rosa Nouchette Carey
Rudyard Kipling
Saint Augustine
Samuel B. Allison
Samuel Hopkins Adams
Sarah Bernhardt
Sarah C. Hallowell
Selma Lagerlof
Sherwood Anderson
Sigmund Freud
Standish O'Grady
Stanley Weyman
Stella Benson
Stella M. Francis

Stephen Crane
Stewart Edward White
Stijn Streuvels
Swami Abhedananda
Swami Parmananda
T. S. Ackland
T. S. Arthur
The Princess Der Ling
Thomas A. Janvier
Thomas A Kempis
Thomas Anderton
Thomas Bailey Aldrich
Thomas Bulfinch
Thomas De Quincey
Thomas Dixon
Thomas H. Huxley
Thomas Hardy
Thomas More
Thornton W. Burgess
U. S. Grant
Upton Sinclair
Valentine Williams
Various Authors
Vaughan Kester
Victor Appleton
Victor G. Durham
Victoria Cross
Virginia Woolf
Wadsworth Camp
Walter Camp
Walter Scott
Washington Irving
Wilbur Lawton
Wilkie Collins
Willa Cather
Willard F. Baker
William Dean Howells
William le Queux
W. Makepeace Thackeray
William W. Walter
William Shakespeare
Winston Churchill
Yei Theodora Ozaki
Yogi Ramacharaka
Young E. Allison
Zane Grey

www.ingramcontent.com/pod-product-compliance
Lightning Source LLC
Chambersburg PA
CBHW050041180626
46810CB00002B/844